CHICAGOLAND DETECTIVE AGENCY

No 4

The Big

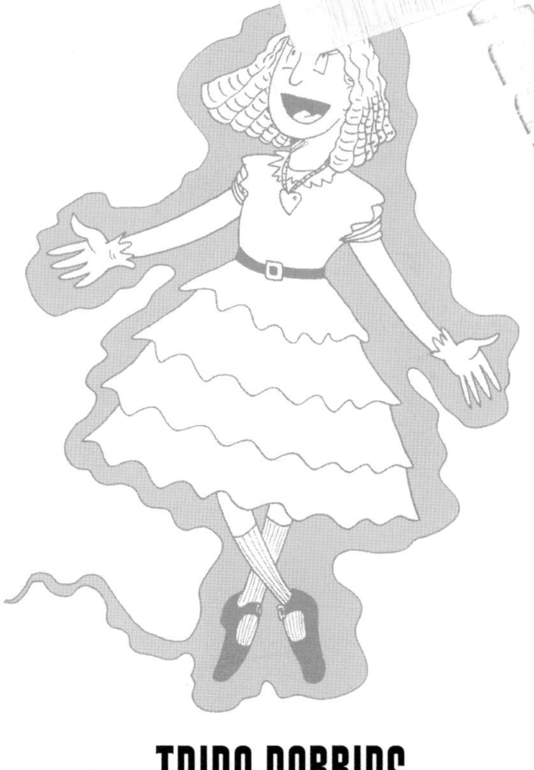

TRINA ROBBINS

ILLUSTRATED BY TYLER PAGE

GRAPHIC UNIVERSE™ • MINNEAPOLIS • NEW YORK

STORY BY TRINA ROBBINS
PENCILS AND INKS BY TYLER PAGE
LETTERING BY ZACK GIALLONGO
COVER COLORING BY HI-FI DESIGN

Copyright © 2012 by Lerner Publishing Group, Inc.

Graphic Universe™ is a trademark of Lerner Publishing Group, Inc.

Graphic Universe™
A division of Lerner Publishing Group, Inc.
241 First Avenue North
Minneapolis, MN 55401 U.S.A.

Website address: www.lernerbooks.com

Library of Congress Cataloging-in-Publication Data

Robbins, Trina.
    The big flush / by Trina Robbins ; illustrated by Tyler Page.
        p.   cm. — (Chicagoland Detective Agency ; #04)
        Summary: Ousted from Stepford Prep, Megan attends a prospective students event with friend Raf and talking dog Bradley at Pine Lake Academy, where Raf is possessed by the spirit of a teenage girl from the 1910s after drinking from an old water fountain.
        ISBN: 978-0-7613-8165-5 (lib. bdg. : alk. paper)
        1. Graphic novels. [1. Graphic novels. 2. Spirit possession—Fiction. 3. Ghosts—Fiction. 4. Schools—Fiction. 5. Dogs—Fiction. 6. Japanese Americans—Fiction.] I. Page, Tyler, 1976- ill. II. Title.
    PZ7.7.R632Big 2012
    741.5'973—dc23   2011044490

Manufactured in the United States of America
1 – PP – 7/15/12

CHAPTER ONE: THE BEGINNING OF THE END

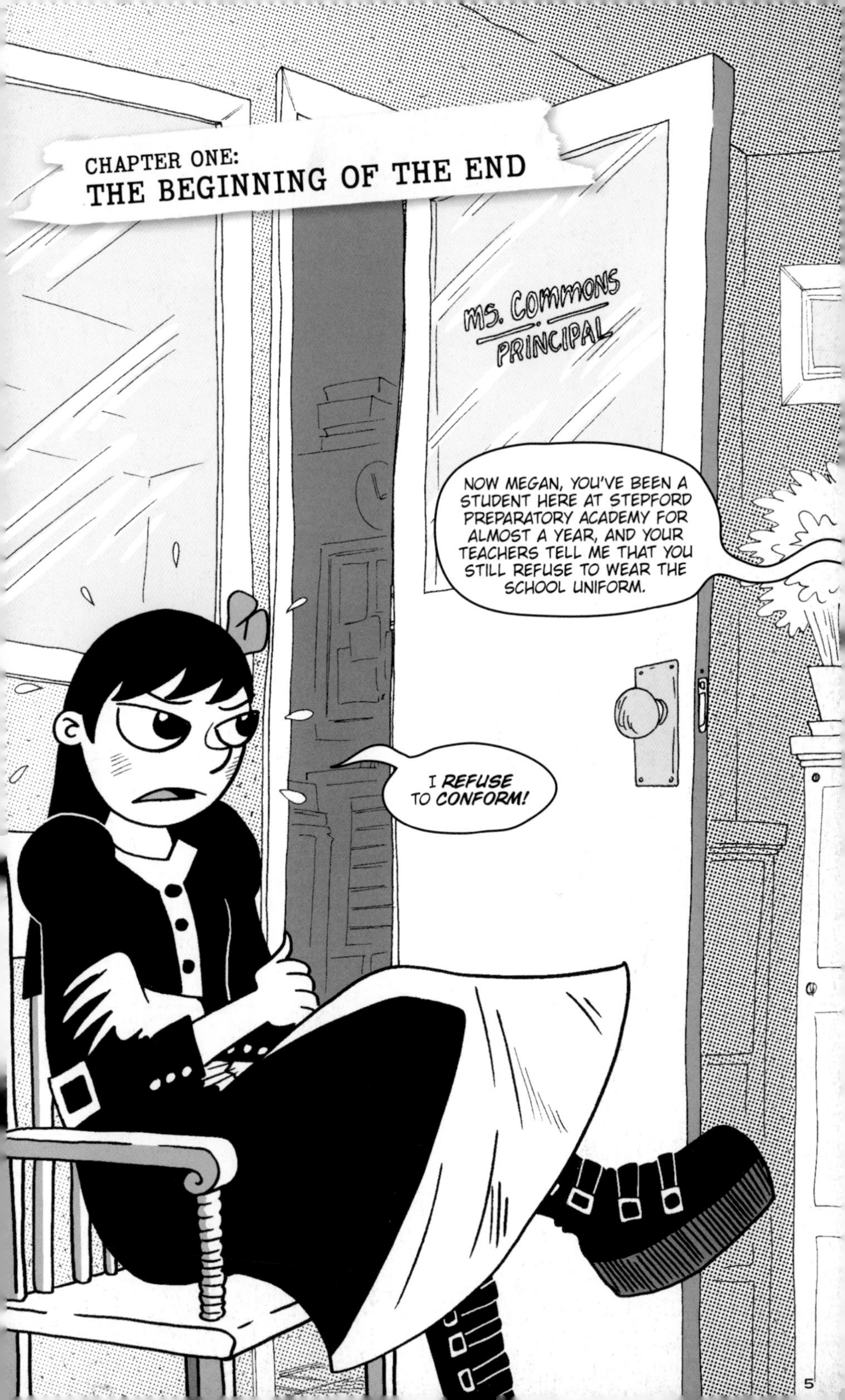
MS. COMMONS PRINCIPAL
NOW MEGAN, YOU'VE BEEN A STUDENT HERE AT STEPFORD PREPARATORY ACADEMY FOR ALMOST A YEAR, AND YOUR TEACHERS TELL ME THAT YOU STILL REFUSE TO WEAR THE SCHOOL UNIFORM.
I *REFUSE* TO *CONFORM!*

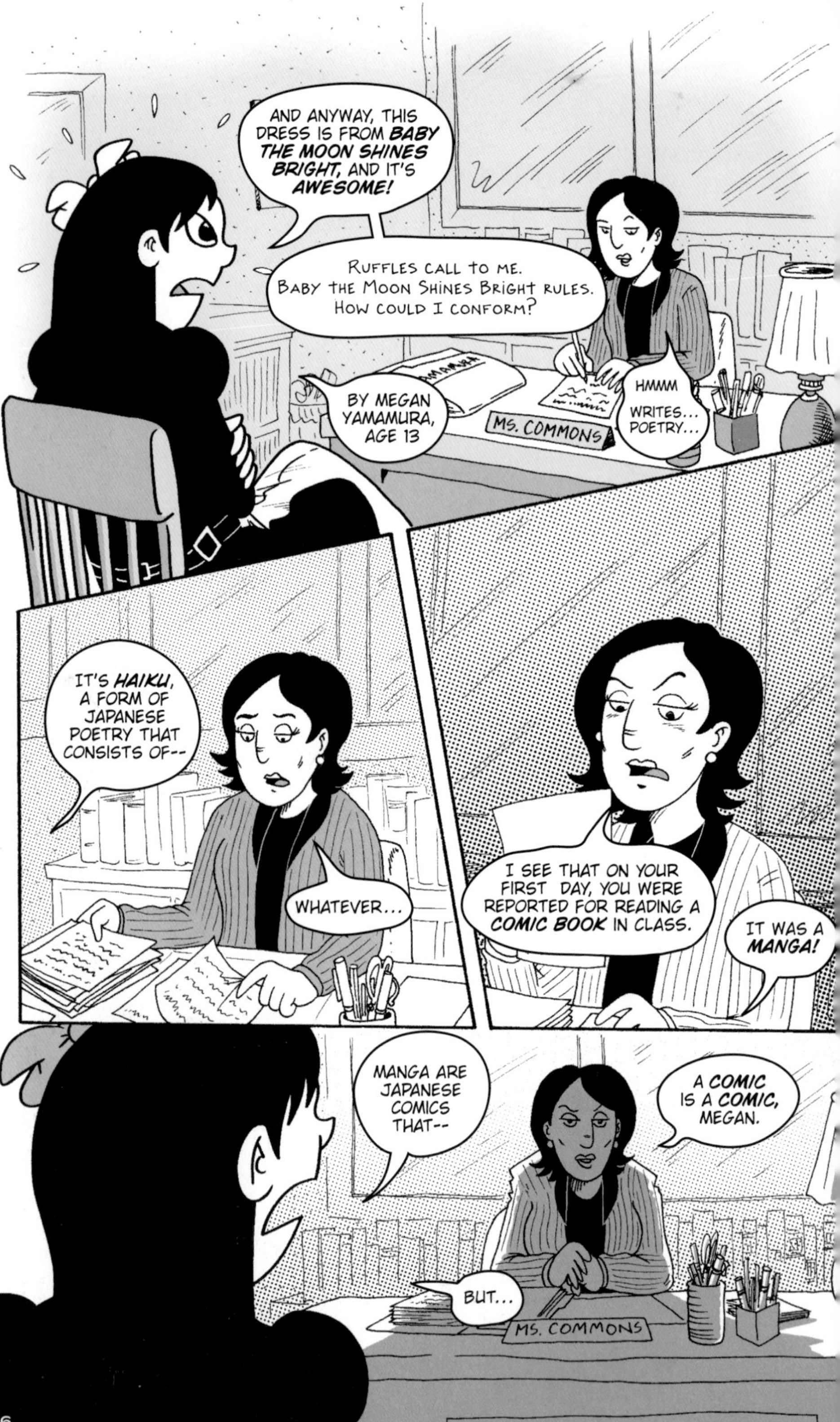
AND ANYWAY, THIS DRESS IS FROM BABY THE MOON SHINES BRIGHT, AND IT'S AWESOME!
RUFFLES CALL TO ME. BABY THE MOON SHINES BRIGHT RULES. HOW COULD I CONFORM?
BY MEGAN YAMAMURA, AGE 13
MS. COMMONS
HMMM
WRITES... POETRY...
IT'S HAIKU, A FORM OF JAPANESE POETRY THAT CONSISTS OF--
WHATEVER...
I SEE THAT ON YOUR FIRST DAY, YOU WERE REPORTED FOR READING A COMIC BOOK IN CLASS.
IT WAS A MANGA!
MANGA ARE JAPANESE COMICS THAT--
A COMIC IS A COMIC, MEGAN.
BUT...
MS. COMMONS

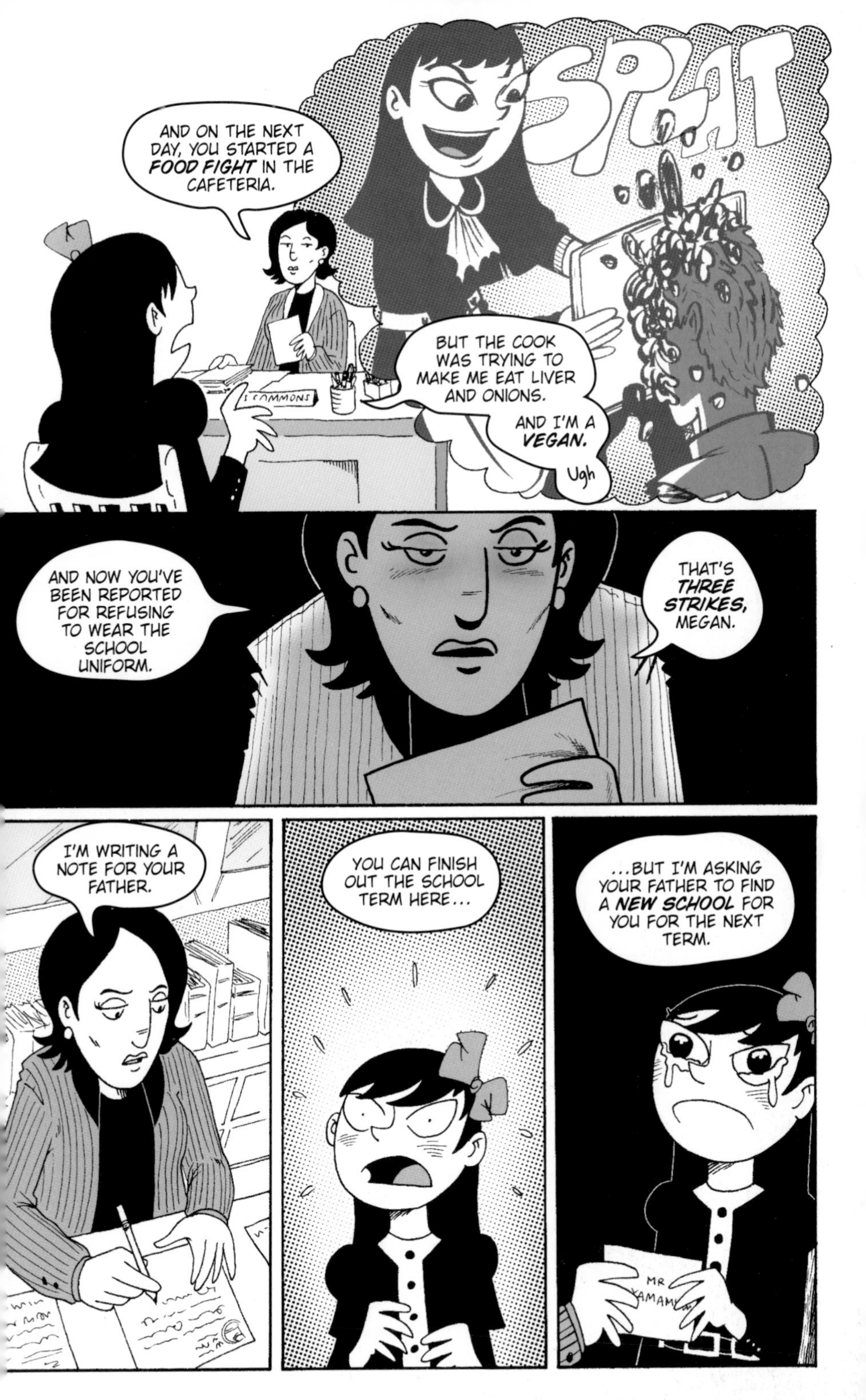

AND ON THE NEXT DAY, YOU STARTED A **FOOD FIGHT** IN THE CAFETERIA.
SPLAT
BUT THE COOK WAS TRYING TO MAKE ME EAT LIVER AND ONIONS.
AND I'M A **VEGAN.**
Ugh
COMMONS
AND NOW YOU'VE BEEN REPORTED FOR REFUSING TO WEAR THE SCHOOL UNIFORM.
THAT'S **THREE STRIKES,** MEGAN.
I'M WRITING A NOTE FOR YOUR FATHER.
YOU CAN FINISH OUT THE SCHOOL TERM HERE...
...BUT I'M ASKING YOUR FATHER TO FIND A **NEW SCHOOL** FOR YOU FOR THE NEXT TERM.
MR YAMAM

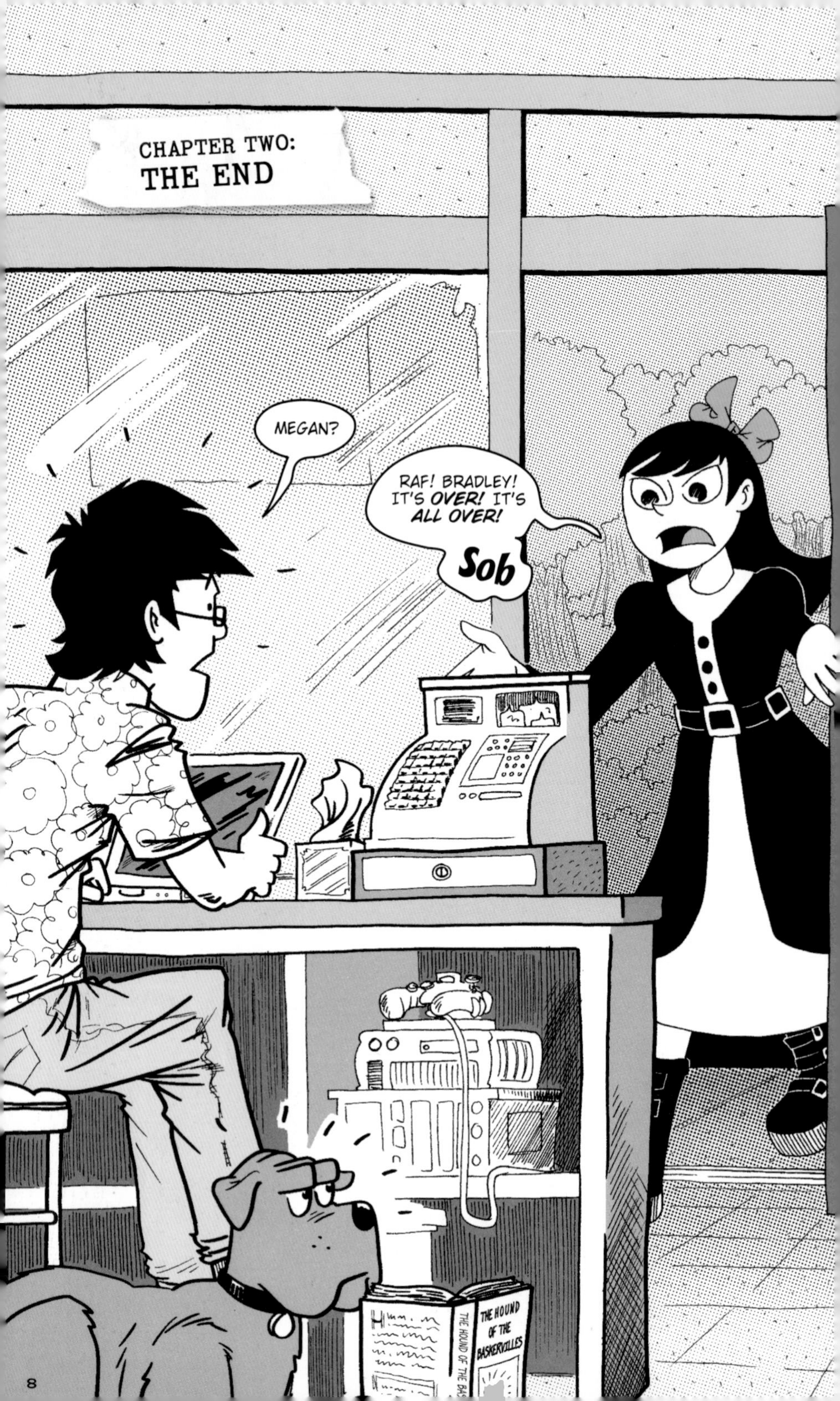

CHAPTER TWO:
THE END
MEGAN?
RAF! BRADLEY! IT'S OVER! IT'S ALL OVER!
Sob
THE HOUND OF THE BASKERVILLES

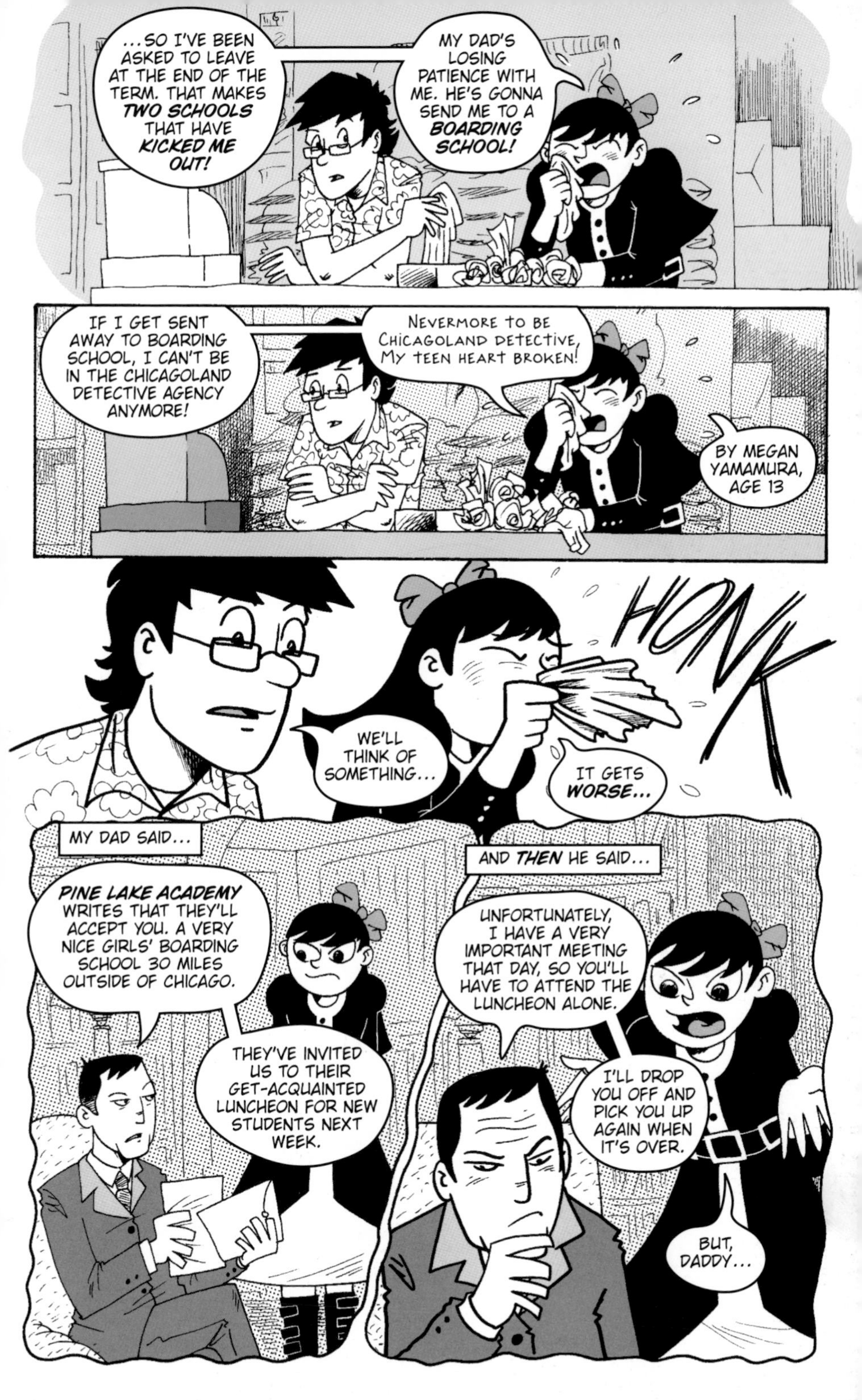
...SO I'VE BEEN ASKED TO LEAVE AT THE END OF THE TERM. THAT MAKES **TWO SCHOOLS** THAT HAVE **KICKED ME OUT!**
MY DAD'S LOSING PATIENCE WITH ME. HE'S GONNA SEND ME TO A **BOARDING SCHOOL!**
IF I GET SENT AWAY TO BOARDING SCHOOL, I CAN'T BE IN THE CHICAGOLAND DETECTIVE AGENCY ANYMORE!
Nevermore to be Chicagoland detective, My teen heart broken!
BY MEGAN YAMAMURA, AGE 13
HONK
WE'LL THINK OF SOMETHING...
IT GETS **WORSE...**
MY DAD SAID...
PINE LAKE ACADEMY WRITES THAT THEY'LL ACCEPT YOU. A VERY NICE GIRLS' BOARDING SCHOOL 30 MILES OUTSIDE OF CHICAGO.
THEY'VE INVITED US TO THEIR GET-ACQUAINTED LUNCHEON FOR NEW STUDENTS NEXT WEEK.
AND **THEN** HE SAID...
UNFORTUNATELY, I HAVE A VERY IMPORTANT MEETING THAT DAY, SO YOU'LL HAVE TO ATTEND THE LUNCHEON ALONE.
I'LL DROP YOU OFF AND PICK YOU UP AGAIN WHEN IT'S OVER.
BUT, DADDY...

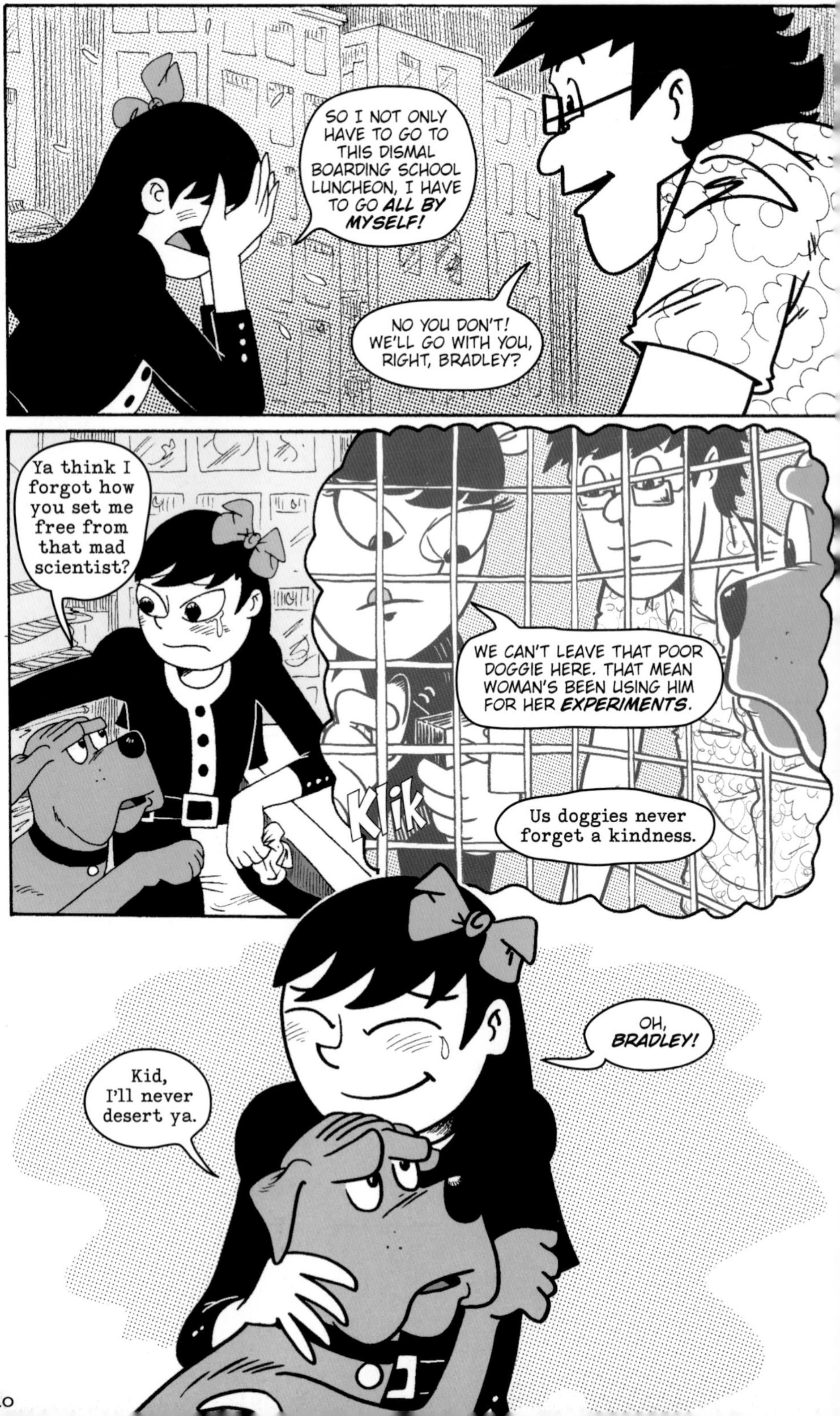
SO I NOT ONLY HAVE TO GO TO THIS DISMAL BOARDING SCHOOL LUNCHEON, I HAVE TO GO ALL BY MYSELF!
NO YOU DON'T! WE'LL GO WITH YOU, RIGHT, BRADLEY?
Ya think I forgot how you set me free from that mad scientist?
WE CAN'T LEAVE THAT POOR DOGGIE HERE. THAT MEAN WOMAN'S BEEN USING HIM FOR HER EXPERIMENTS.
KLIK
Us doggies never forget a kindness.
OH, BRADLEY!
Kid, I'll never desert ya.

CHAPTER THREE:
CALL THE PLUMBER!

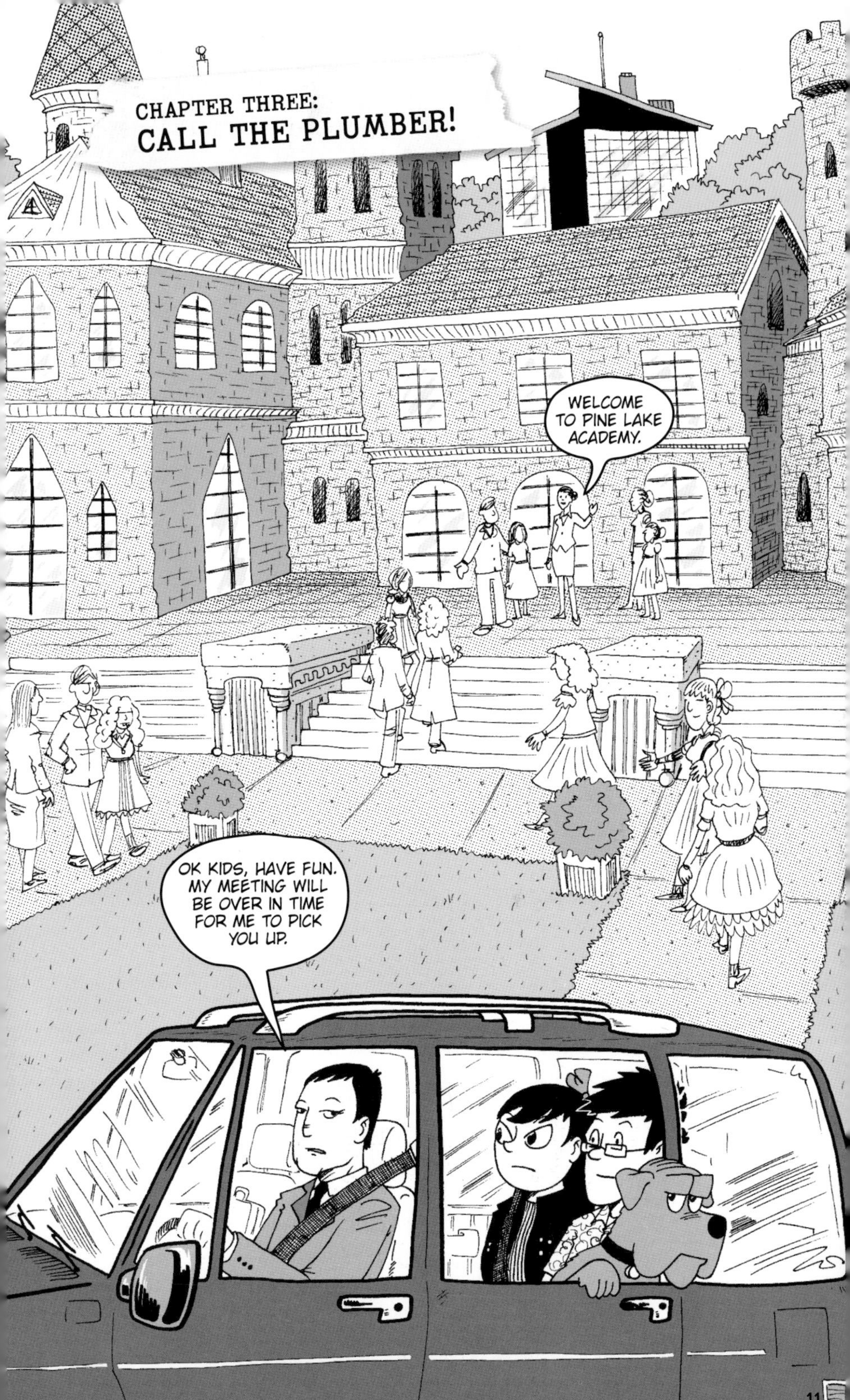
WELCOME TO PINE LAKE ACADEMY.
OK KIDS, HAVE FUN. MY MEETING WILL BE OVER IN TIME FOR ME TO PICK YOU UP.

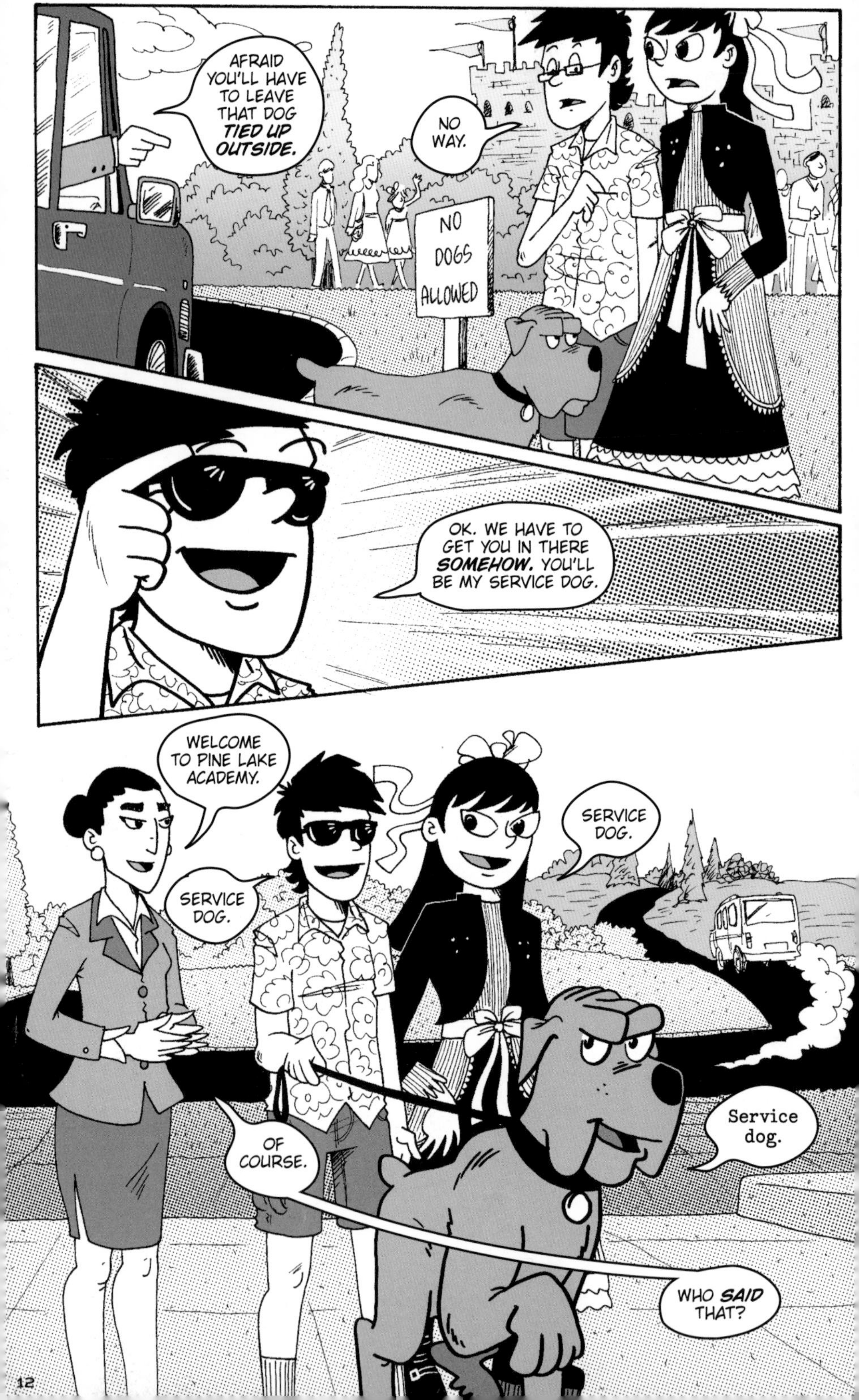

AFRAID YOU'LL HAVE TO LEAVE THAT DOG *TIED UP OUTSIDE.*
NO WAY.
NO DOGS ALLOWED
OK. WE HAVE TO GET YOU IN THERE *SOMEHOW.* YOU'LL BE MY SERVICE DOG.
WELCOME TO PINE LAKE ACADEMY.
SERVICE DOG.
SERVICE DOG.
Service dog.
OF COURSE.
WHO *SAID* THAT?

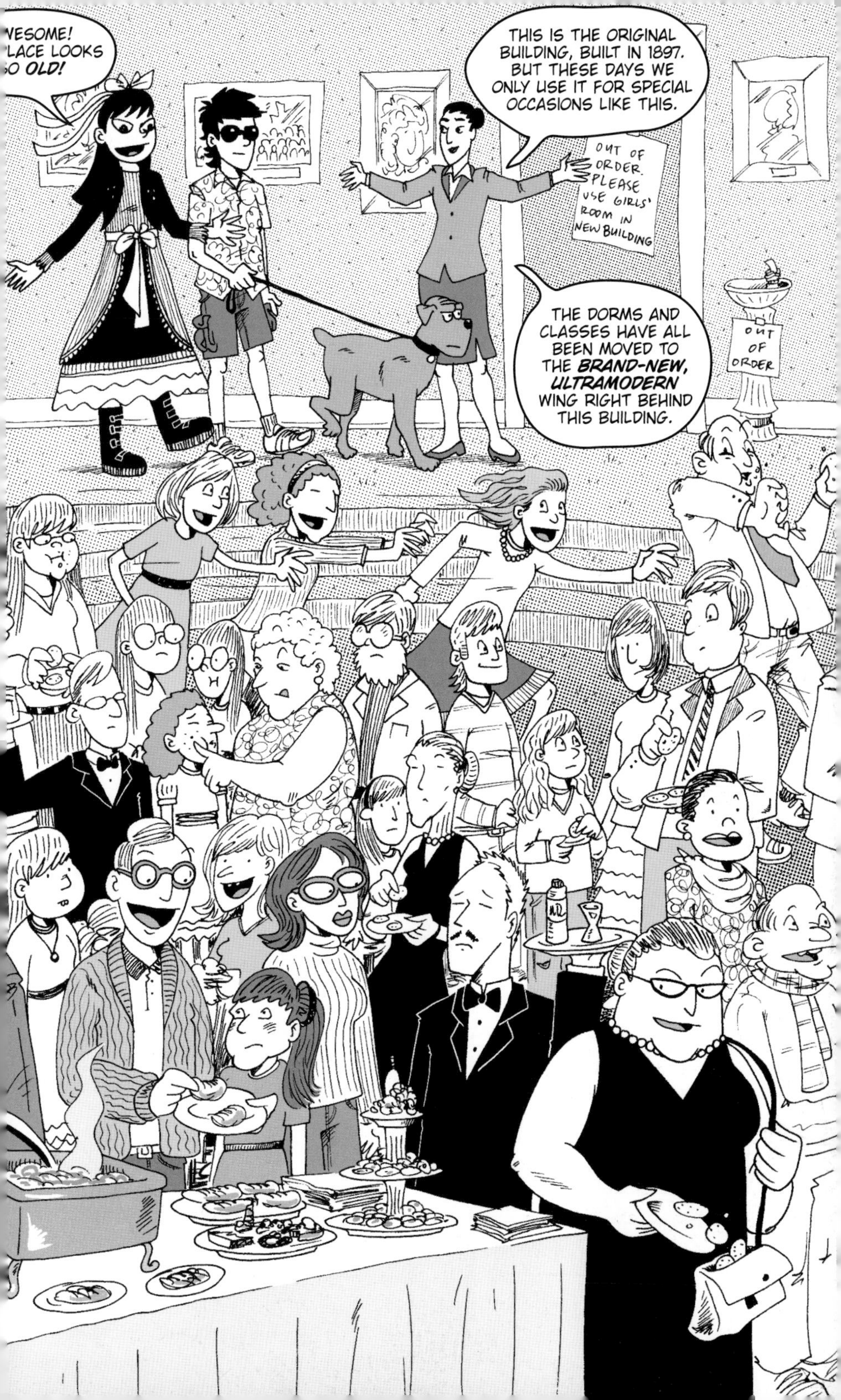

WESOME! PLACE LOOKS SO OLD!
THIS IS THE ORIGINAL BUILDING, BUILT IN 1897. BUT THESE DAYS WE ONLY USE IT FOR SPECIAL OCCASIONS LIKE THIS.
OUT OF ORDER. PLEASE USE GIRLS' ROOM IN NEW BUILDING
THE DORMS AND CLASSES HAVE ALL BEEN MOVED TO THE BRAND-NEW, ULTRAMODERN WING RIGHT BEHIND THIS BUILDING.
OUT OF ORDER

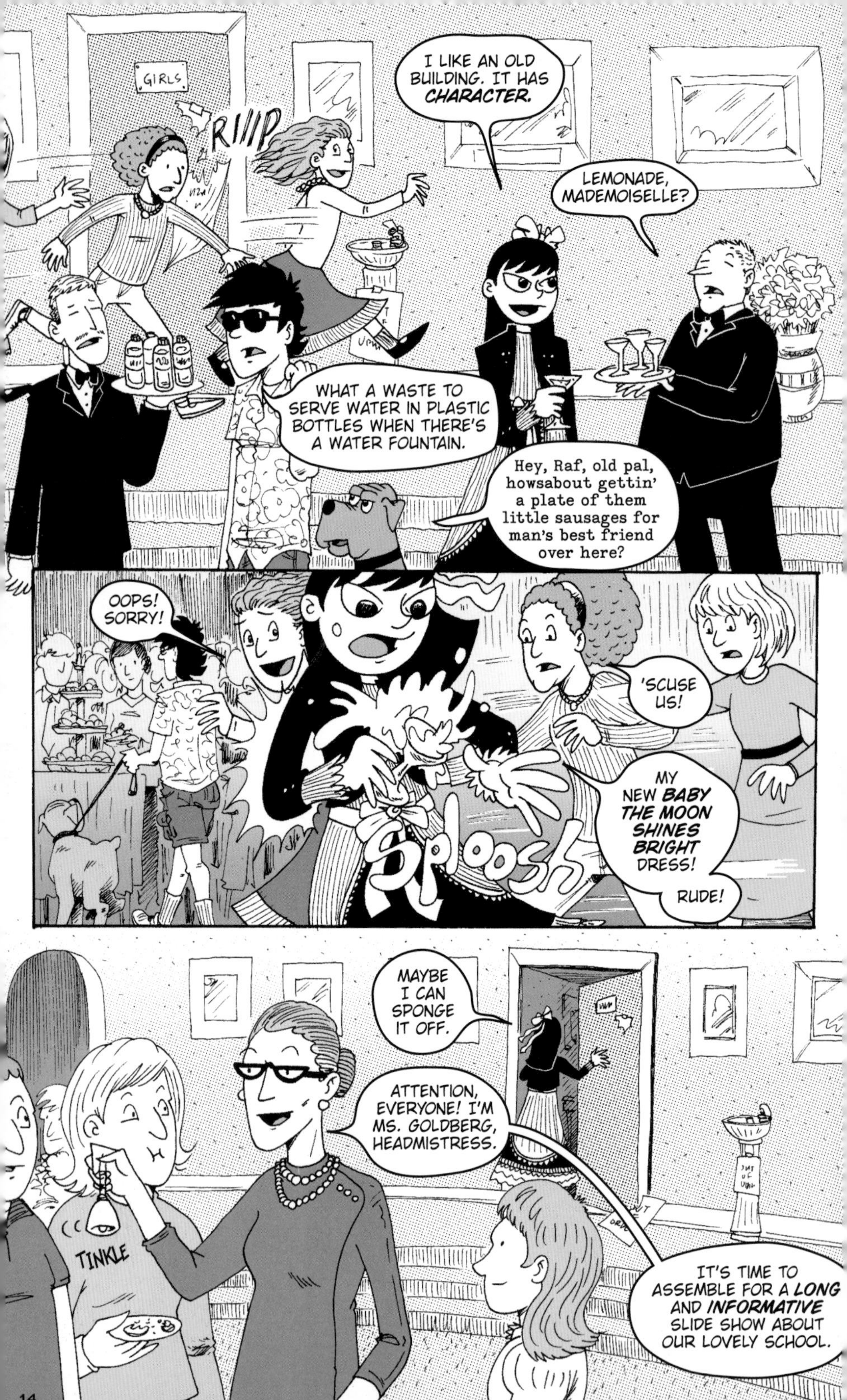
GIRLS
RIIIP
I LIKE AN OLD BUILDING. IT HAS *CHARACTER.*
LEMONADE, MADEMOISELLE?
WHAT A WASTE TO SERVE WATER IN PLASTIC BOTTLES WHEN THERE'S A WATER FOUNTAIN.
Hey, Raf, old pal, howsabout gettin' a plate of them little sausages for man's best friend over here?
OOPS! SORRY!
'SCUSE US!
Sploosh
MY NEW ***BABY THE MOON SHINES BRIGHT*** DRESS!
RUDE!
MAYBE I CAN SPONGE IT OFF.
ATTENTION, EVERYONE! I'M MS. GOLDBERG, HEADMISTRESS.
TINKLE
IT'S TIME TO ASSEMBLE FOR A ***LONG*** AND ***INFORMATIVE*** SLIDE SHOW ABOUT OUR LOVELY SCHOOL.

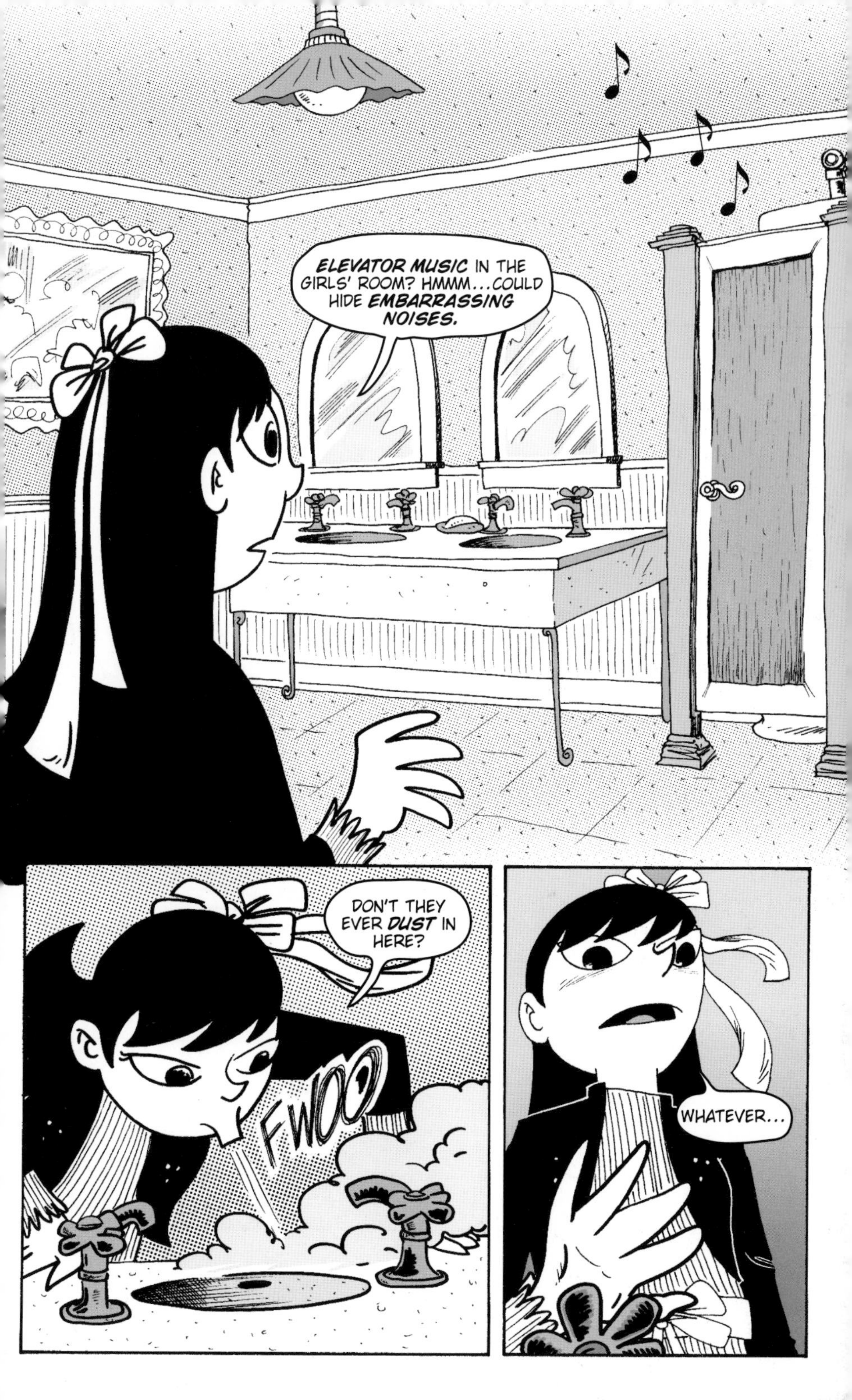
ELEVATOR MUSIC IN THE GIRLS' ROOM? HMMM...COULD HIDE EMBARRASSING NOISES.
DON'T THEY EVER DUST IN HERE?
FWOO
WHATEVER...

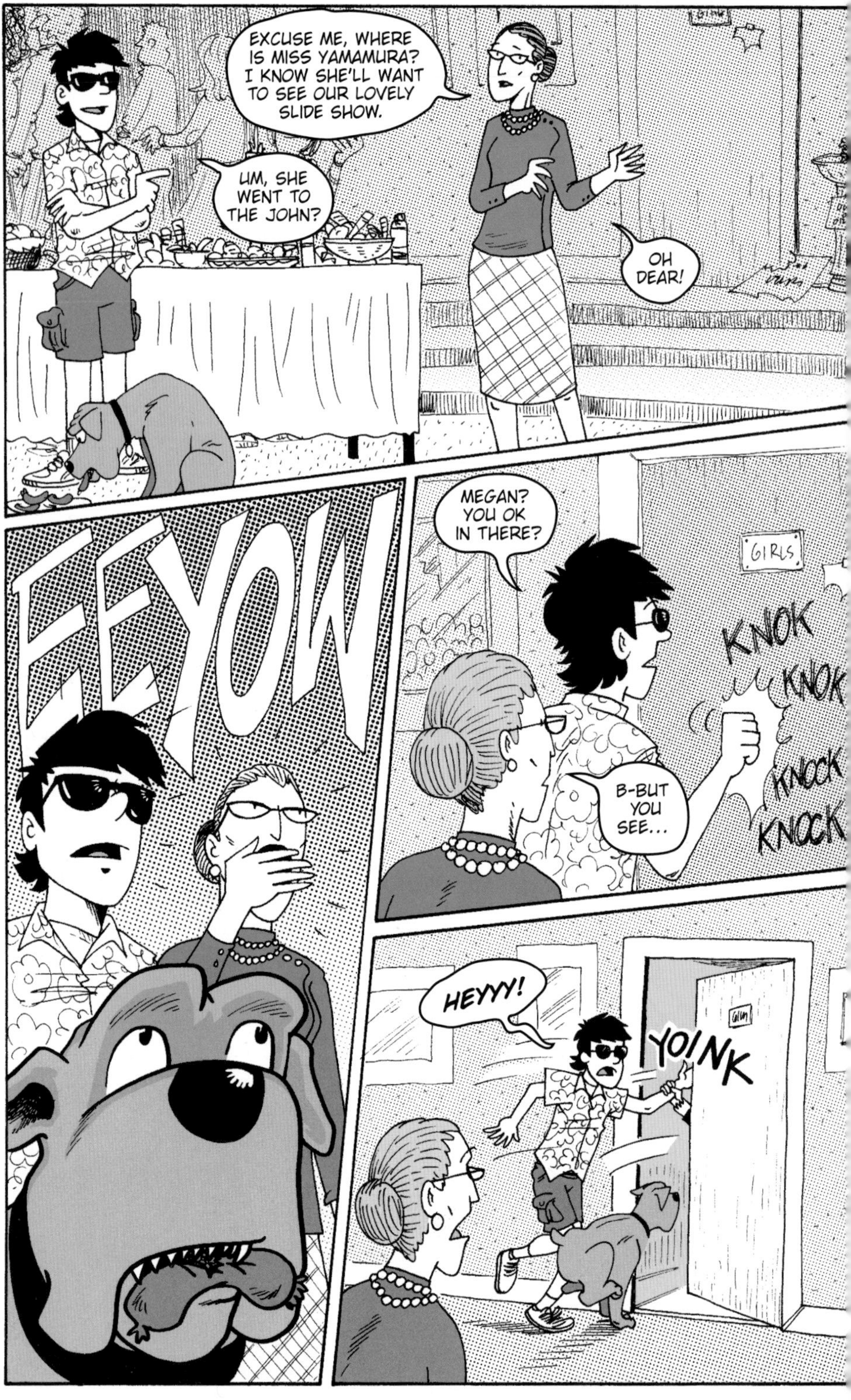
EXCUSE ME, WHERE IS MISS YAMAMURA? I KNOW SHE'LL WANT TO SEE OUR LOVELY SLIDE SHOW.
UM, SHE WENT TO THE JOHN?
OH DEAR!
EEYOW
MEGAN? YOU OK IN THERE?
GIRLS
KNOK
KNOK
KNOCK
KNOCK
B-BUT YOU SEE...
HEYYY!
YOINK

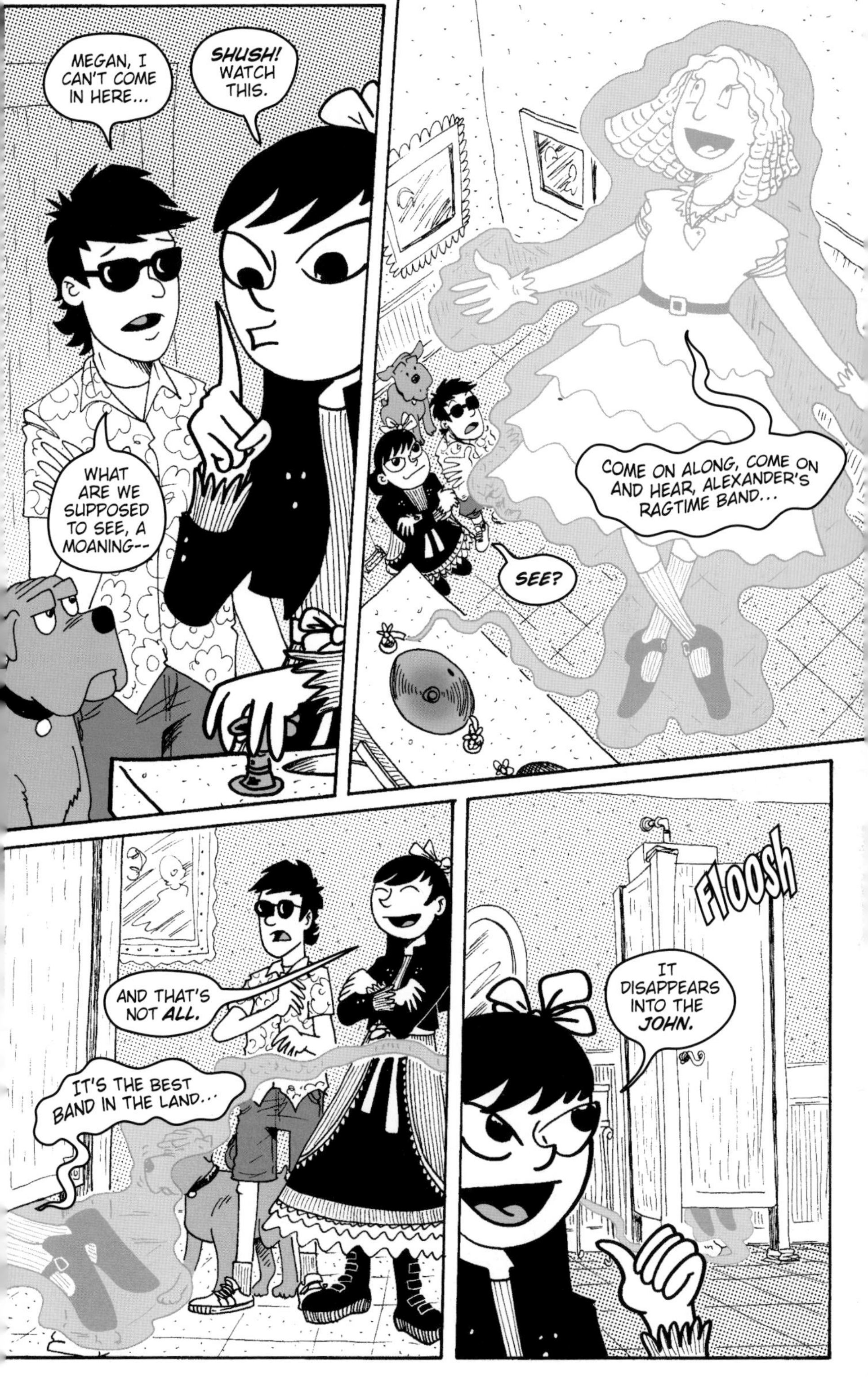
MEGAN, I CAN'T COME IN HERE...
SHUSH! WATCH THIS.
WHAT ARE WE SUPPOSED TO SEE, A MOANING--
COME ON ALONG, COME ON AND HEAR, ALEXANDER'S RAGTIME BAND...
SEE?
AND THAT'S NOT ***ALL.***
IT'S THE BEST BAND IN THE LAND...
FLOOSH
IT DISAPPEARS INTO THE ***JOHN.***

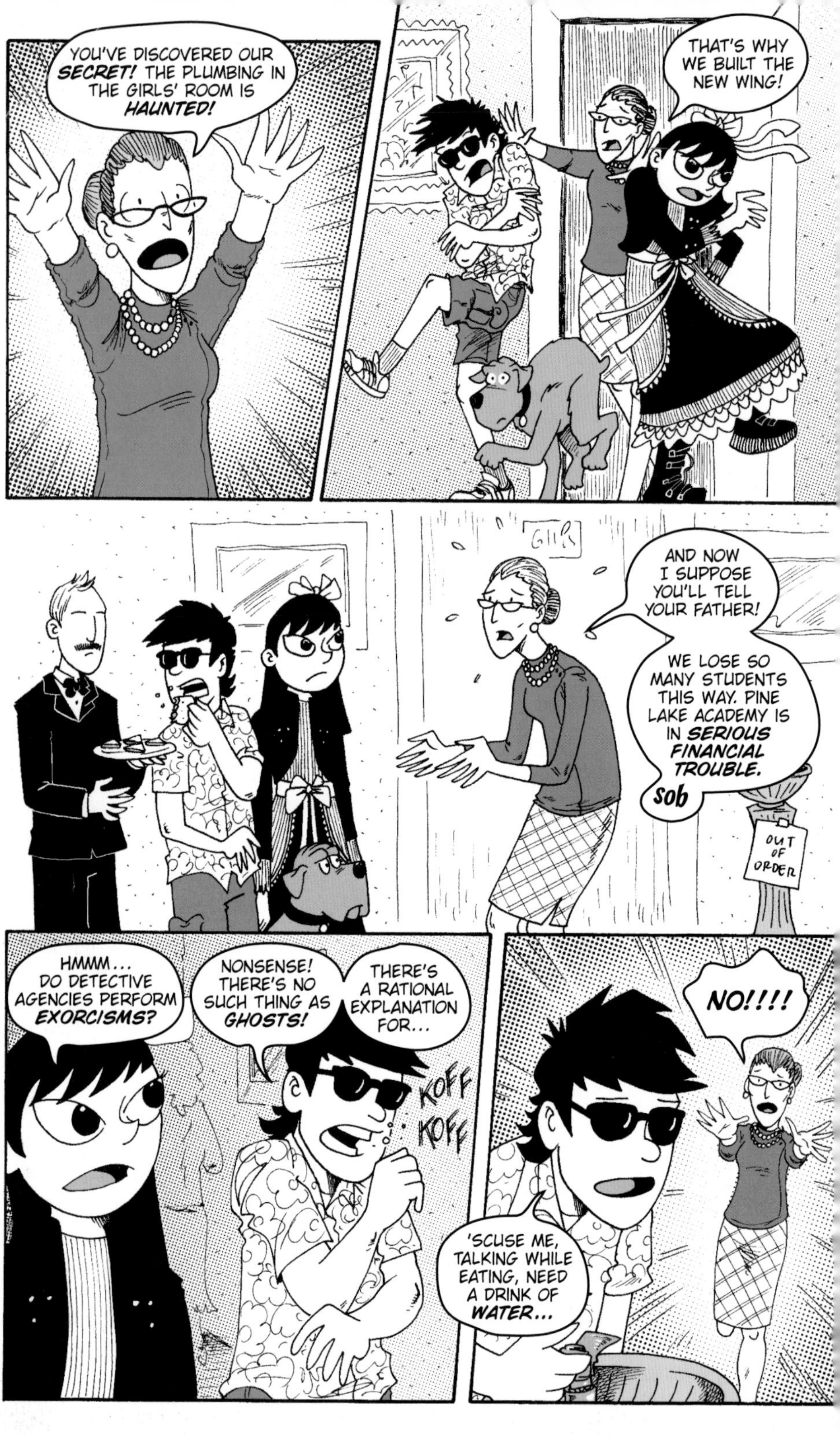
YOU'VE DISCOVERED OUR SECRET! THE PLUMBING IN THE GIRLS' ROOM IS HAUNTED!
THAT'S WHY WE BUILT THE NEW WING!
AND NOW I SUPPOSE YOU'LL TELL YOUR FATHER!
WE LOSE SO MANY STUDENTS THIS WAY. PINE LAKE ACADEMY IS IN SERIOUS FINANCIAL TROUBLE.
sob
OUT OF ORDER
HMMM... DO DETECTIVE AGENCIES PERFORM EXORCISMS?
NONSENSE! THERE'S NO SUCH THING AS GHOSTS!
THERE'S A RATIONAL EXPLANATION FOR...
KOFF KOFF
NO!!!!
'SCUSE ME, TALKING WHILE EATING, NEED A DRINK OF WATER...

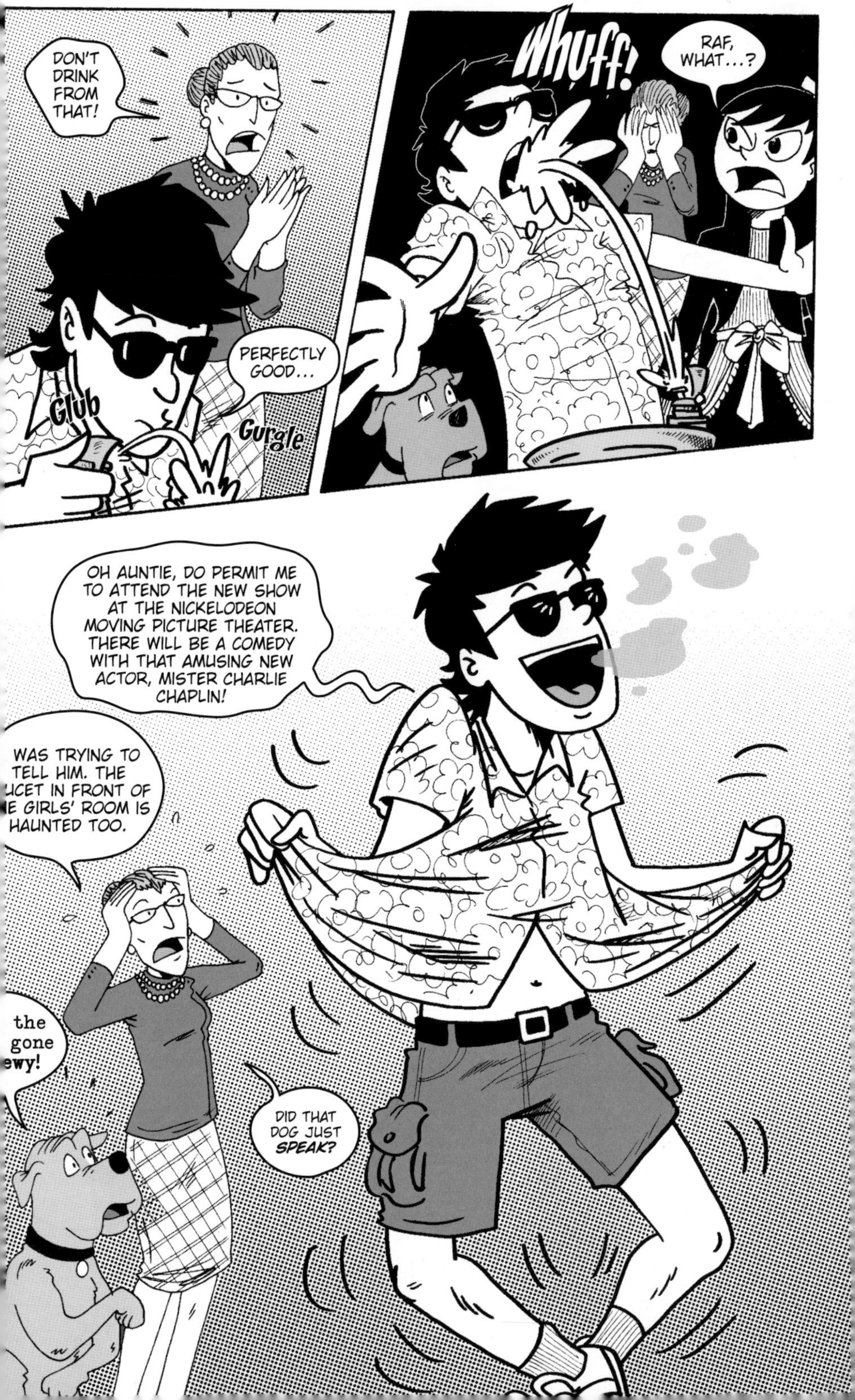
DON'T DRINK FROM THAT!
GLUB
PERFECTLY GOOD...
GURGLE
WHUFF!
RAF, WHAT...?
OH AUNTIE, DO PERMIT ME TO ATTEND THE NEW SHOW AT THE NICKELODEON MOVING PICTURE THEATER. THERE WILL BE A COMEDY WITH THAT AMUSING NEW ACTOR, MISTER CHARLIE CHAPLIN!
WAS TRYING TO TELL HIM. THE UCET IN FRONT OF E GIRLS' ROOM IS HAUNTED TOO.
the gone ewy!
DID THAT DOG JUST SPEAK?

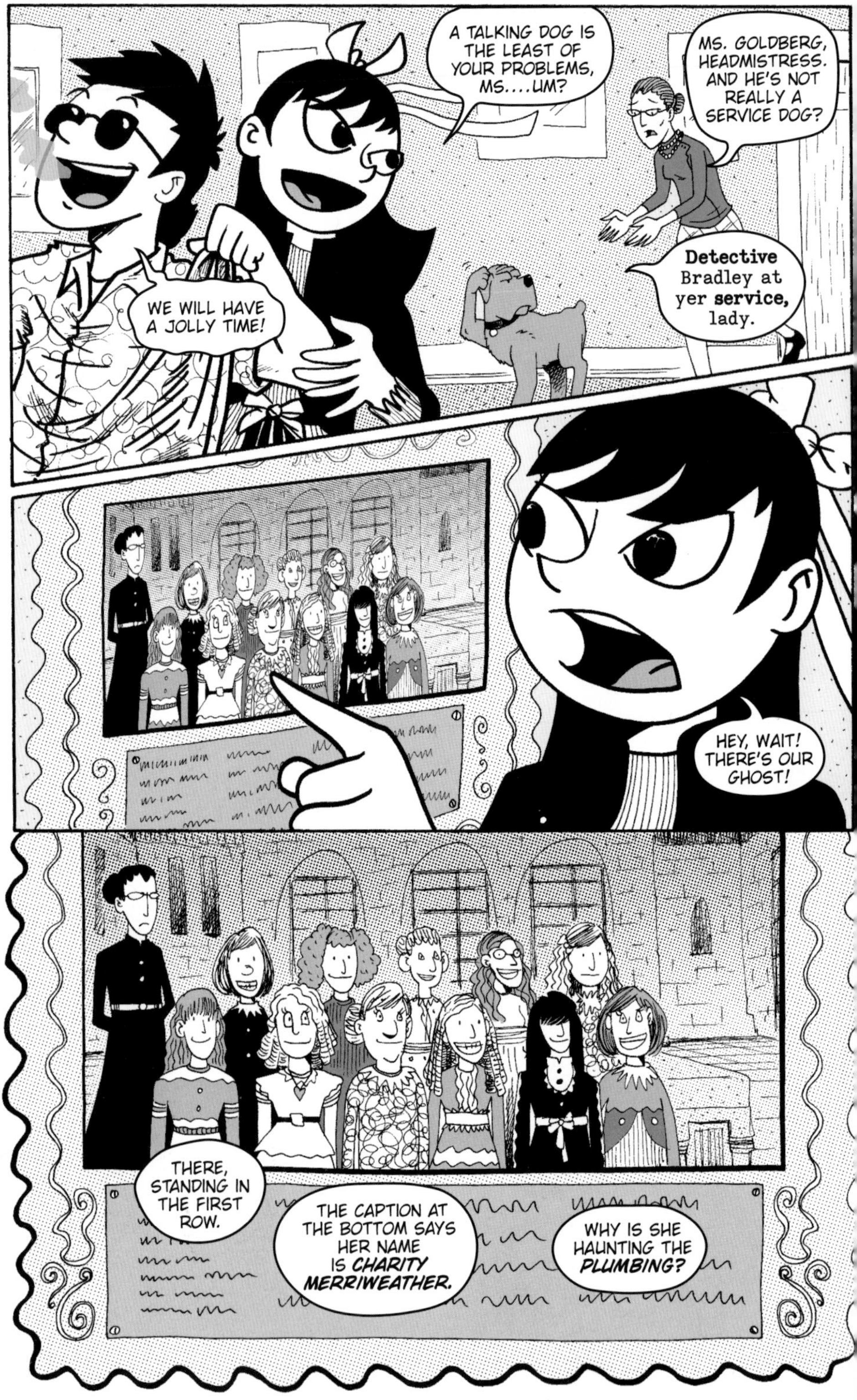
WE WILL HAVE A JOLLY TIME!
A TALKING DOG IS THE LEAST OF YOUR PROBLEMS, MS.... UM?
MS. GOLDBERG, HEADMISTRESS. AND HE'S NOT REALLY A SERVICE DOG?
Detective Bradley at yer **service,** lady.
HEY, WAIT! THERE'S OUR GHOST!
THERE, STANDING IN THE FIRST ROW.
THE CAPTION AT THE BOTTOM SAYS HER NAME IS ***CHARITY MERRIWEATHER.***
WHY IS SHE HAUNTING THE ***PLUMBING?***

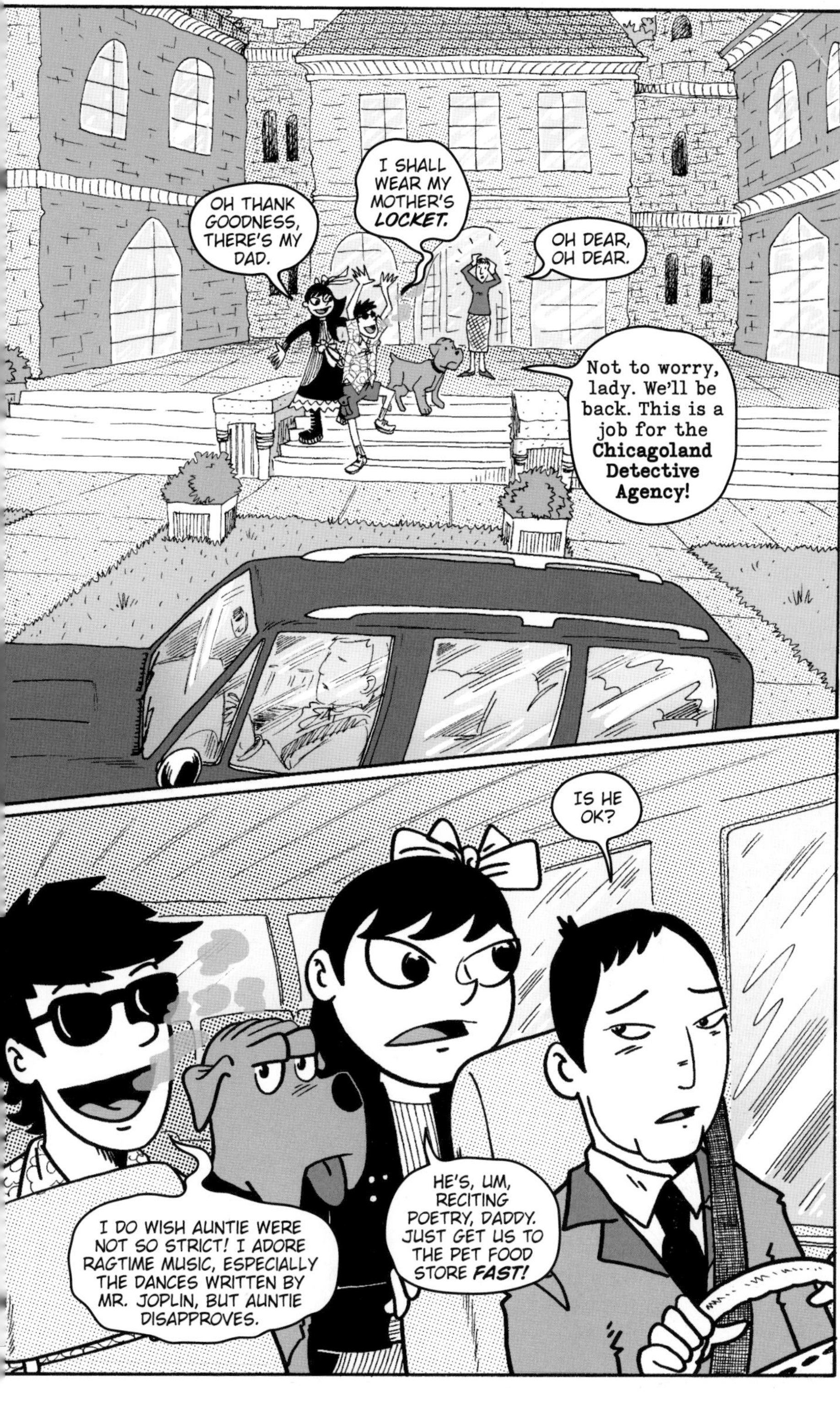
OH THANK GOODNESS, THERE'S MY DAD.
I SHALL WEAR MY MOTHER'S LOCKET.
OH DEAR, OH DEAR.
Not to worry, lady. We'll be back. This is a job for the Chicagoland Detective Agency!
IS HE OK?
I DO WISH AUNTIE WERE NOT SO STRICT! I ADORE RAGTIME MUSIC, ESPECIALLY THE DANCES WRITTEN BY MR. JOPLIN, BUT AUNTIE DISAPPROVES.
HE'S, UM, RECITING POETRY, DADDY. JUST GET US TO THE PET FOOD STORE FAST!

CHAPTER FOUR:
THE GHOST CHANNEL

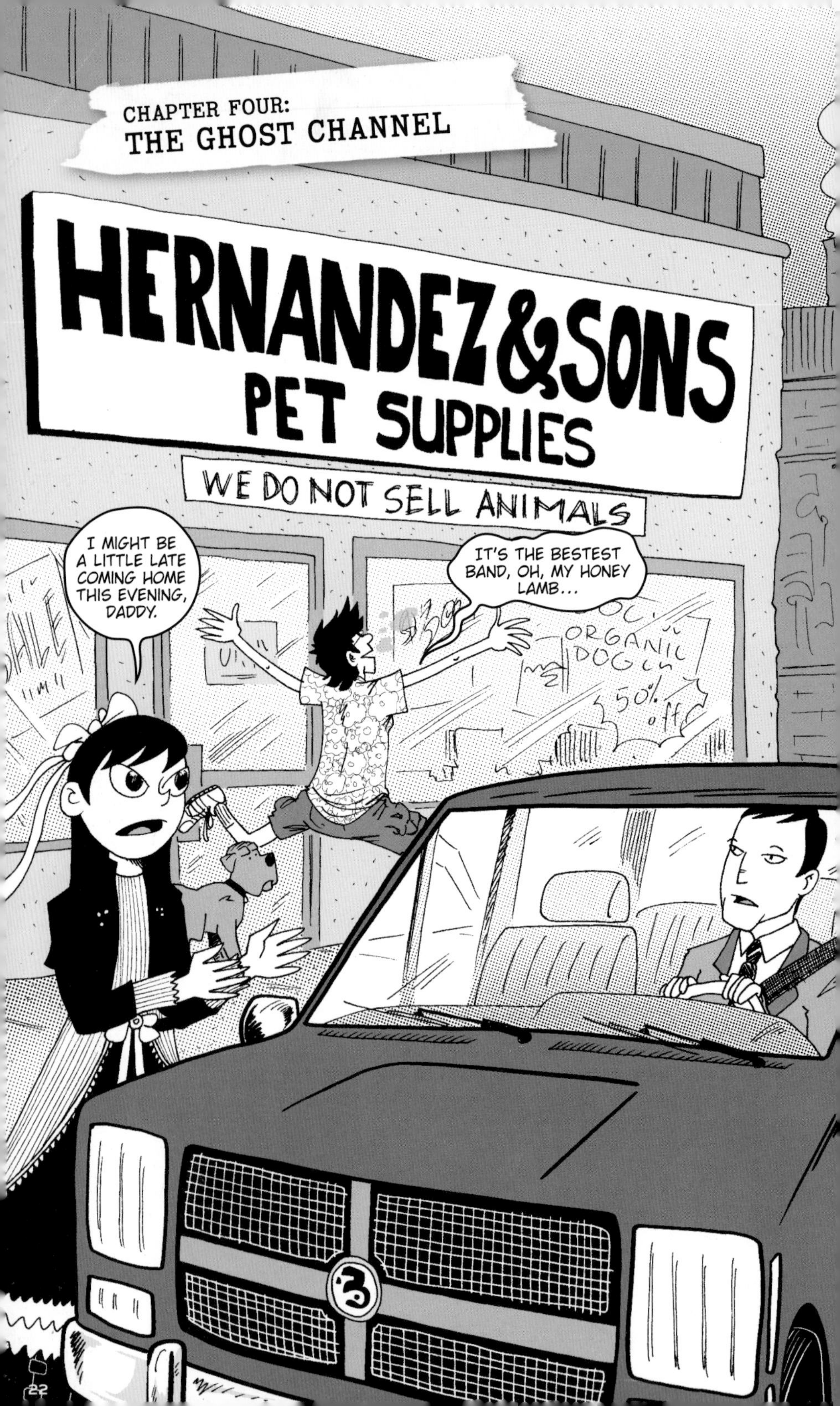

HERNANDEZ & SONS
PET SUPPLIES
WE DO NOT SELL ANIMALS
I MIGHT BE A LITTLE LATE COMING HOME THIS EVENING, DADDY.
IT'S THE BESTEST BAND, OH, MY HONEY LAMB...
ORGANIC DOG
50% off

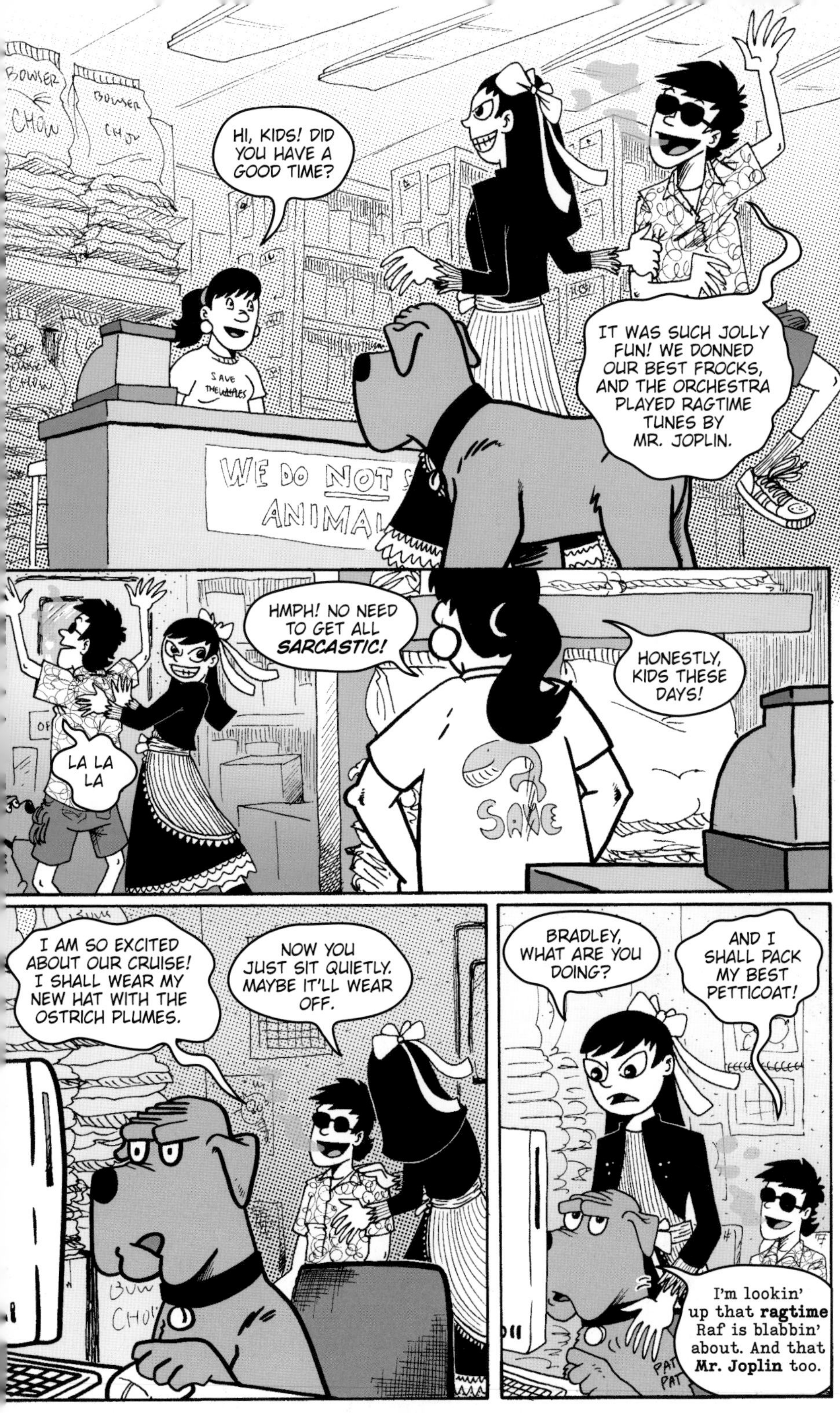

BOWSER CHOW
BOWSER CHOW
HI, KIDS! DID YOU HAVE A GOOD TIME?
IT WAS SUCH JOLLY FUN! WE DONNED OUR BEST FROCKS, AND THE ORCHESTRA PLAYED RAGTIME TUNES BY MR. JOPLIN.
SAVE THE WHALES
WE DO NOT
ANIMAL
HMPH! NO NEED TO GET ALL SARCASTIC!
HONESTLY, KIDS THESE DAYS!
LA LA LA
SAVE
I AM SO EXCITED ABOUT OUR CRUISE! I SHALL WEAR MY NEW HAT WITH THE OSTRICH PLUMES.
NOW YOU JUST SIT QUIETLY. MAYBE IT'LL WEAR OFF.
BRADLEY, WHAT ARE YOU DOING?
AND I SHALL PACK MY BEST PETTICOAT!
I'm lookin' up that **ragtime** Raf is blabbin' about. And that **Mr. Joplin** too.
PAT PAT

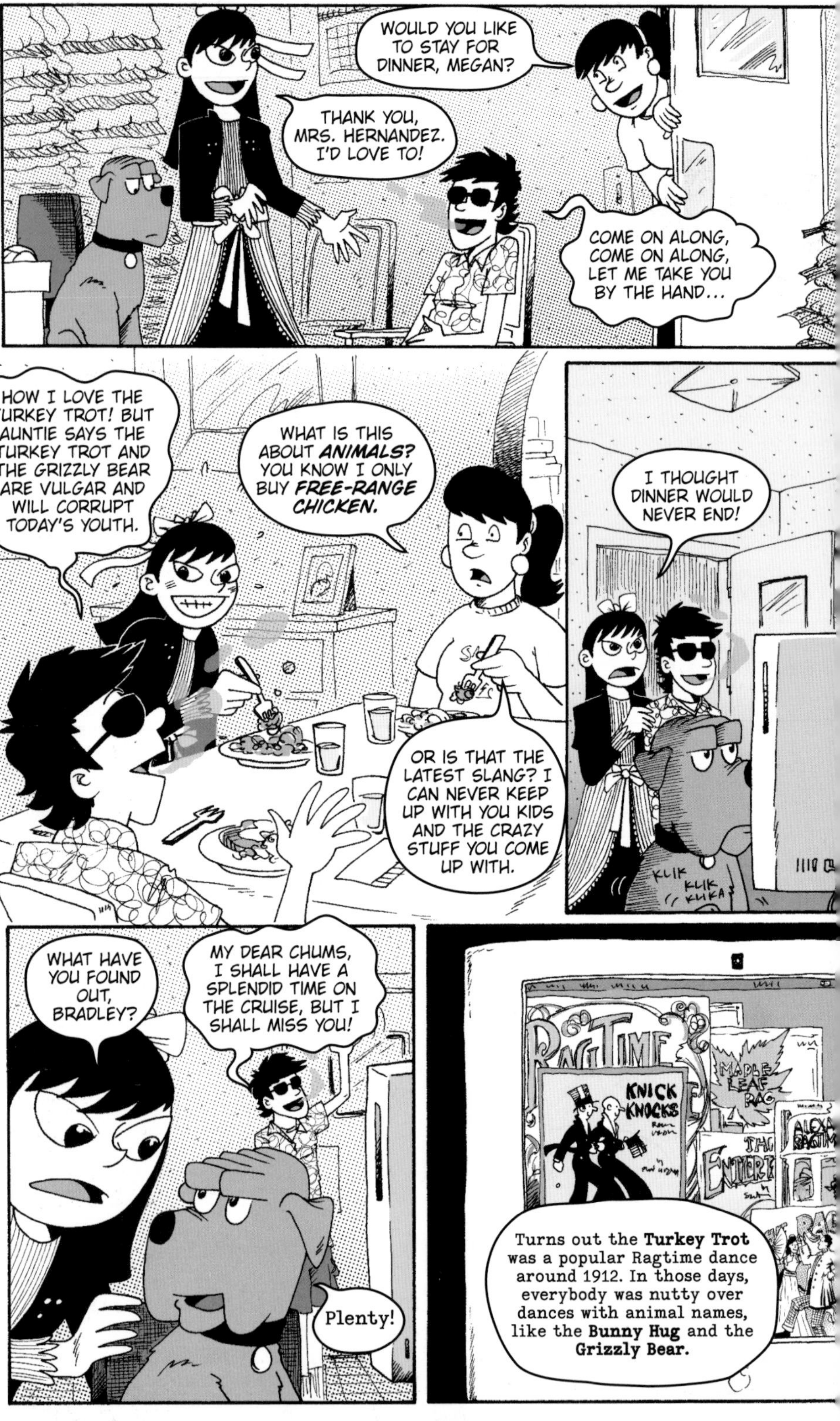
WOULD YOU LIKE TO STAY FOR DINNER, MEGAN?
THANK YOU, MRS. HERNANDEZ. I'D LOVE TO!
COME ON ALONG, COME ON ALONG, LET ME TAKE YOU BY THE HAND...
HOW I LOVE THE TURKEY TROT! BUT AUNTIE SAYS THE TURKEY TROT AND THE GRIZZLY BEAR ARE VULGAR AND WILL CORRUPT TODAY'S YOUTH.
WHAT IS THIS ABOUT ***ANIMALS?*** YOU KNOW I ONLY BUY ***FREE-RANGE CHICKEN.***
OR IS THAT THE LATEST SLANG? I CAN NEVER KEEP UP WITH YOU KIDS AND THE CRAZY STUFF YOU COME UP WITH.
I THOUGHT DINNER WOULD NEVER END!
KLIK
KLIK
KLIKA
WHAT HAVE YOU FOUND OUT, BRADLEY?
MY DEAR CHUMS, I SHALL HAVE A SPLENDID TIME ON THE CRUISE, BUT I SHALL MISS YOU!
Plenty!
KNICK KNOCKS
MAPLE LEAF RAG
Turns out the **Turkey Trot** was a popular Ragtime dance around 1912. In those days, everybody was nutty over dances with animal names, like the **Bunny Hug** and the **Grizzly Bear.**

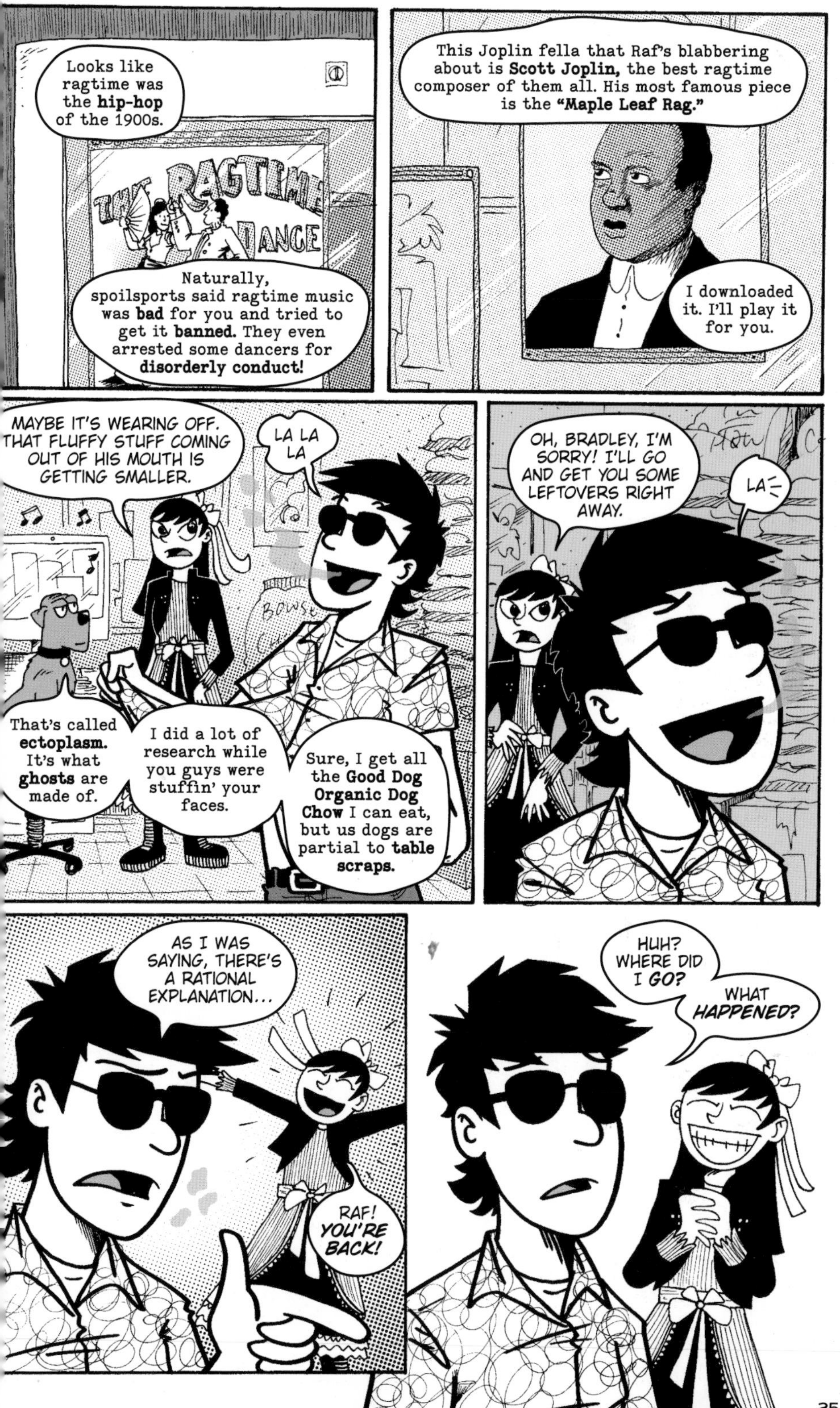

Looks like ragtime was the **hip-hop** of the 1900s.
Naturally, spoilsports said ragtime music was **bad** for you and tried to get it **banned.** They even arrested some dancers for **disorderly conduct!**
This Joplin fella that Raf's blabbering about is **Scott Joplin,** the best ragtime composer of them all. His most famous piece is the **"Maple Leaf Rag."**
I downloaded it. I'll play it for you.
MAYBE IT'S WEARING OFF. THAT FLUFFY STUFF COMING OUT OF HIS MOUTH IS GETTING SMALLER.
LA LA LA
That's called **ectoplasm.** It's what **ghosts** are made of.
I did a lot of research while you guys were stuffin' your faces.
Sure, I get all the **Good Dog Organic Dog Chow** I can eat, but us dogs are partial to **table scraps.**
OH, BRADLEY, I'M SORRY! I'LL GO AND GET YOU SOME LEFTOVERS RIGHT AWAY.
LA
AS I WAS SAYING, THERE'S A RATIONAL EXPLANATION...
RAF! *YOU'RE BACK!*
HUH? WHERE DID I *GO?*
WHAT *HAPPENED?*

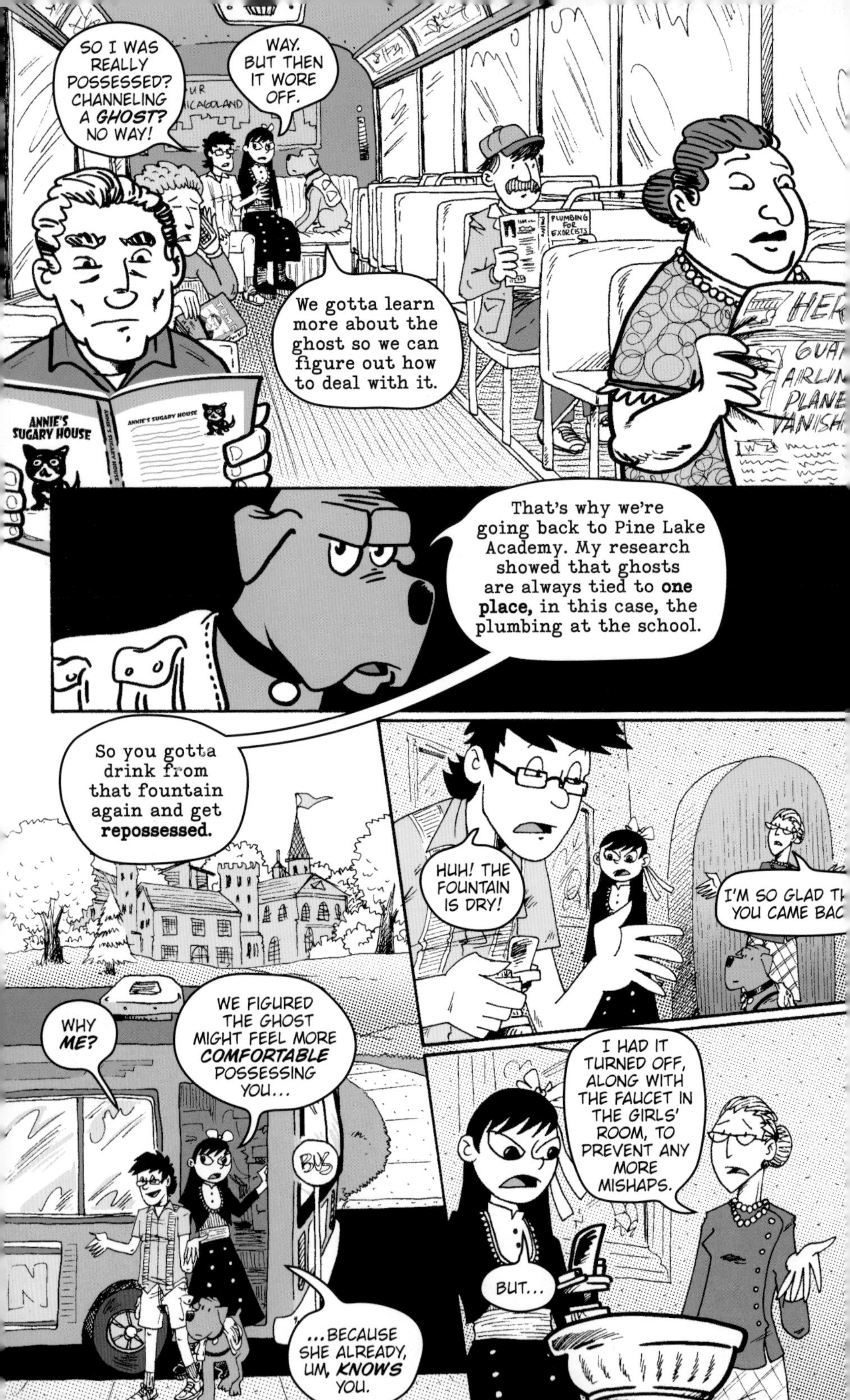
SO I WAS REALLY POSSESSED? CHANNELING A GHOST? NO WAY!
WAY. BUT THEN IT WORE OFF.
We gotta learn more about the ghost so we can figure out how to deal with it.
PLUMBING FOR EXORCISTS
ANNIE'S SUGARY HOUSE
That's why we're going back to Pine Lake Academy. My research showed that ghosts are always tied to one place, in this case, the plumbing at the school.
So you gotta drink from that fountain again and get repossessed.
WHY ME?
WE FIGURED THE GHOST MIGHT FEEL MORE COMFORTABLE POSSESSING YOU...
...BECAUSE SHE ALREADY, UM, KNOWS YOU.
BUS
HUH! THE FOUNTAIN IS DRY!
I'M SO GLAD T YOU CAME BAC
I HAD IT TURNED OFF, ALONG WITH THE FAUCET IN THE GIRLS' ROOM, TO PREVENT ANY MORE MISHAPS.
BUT...

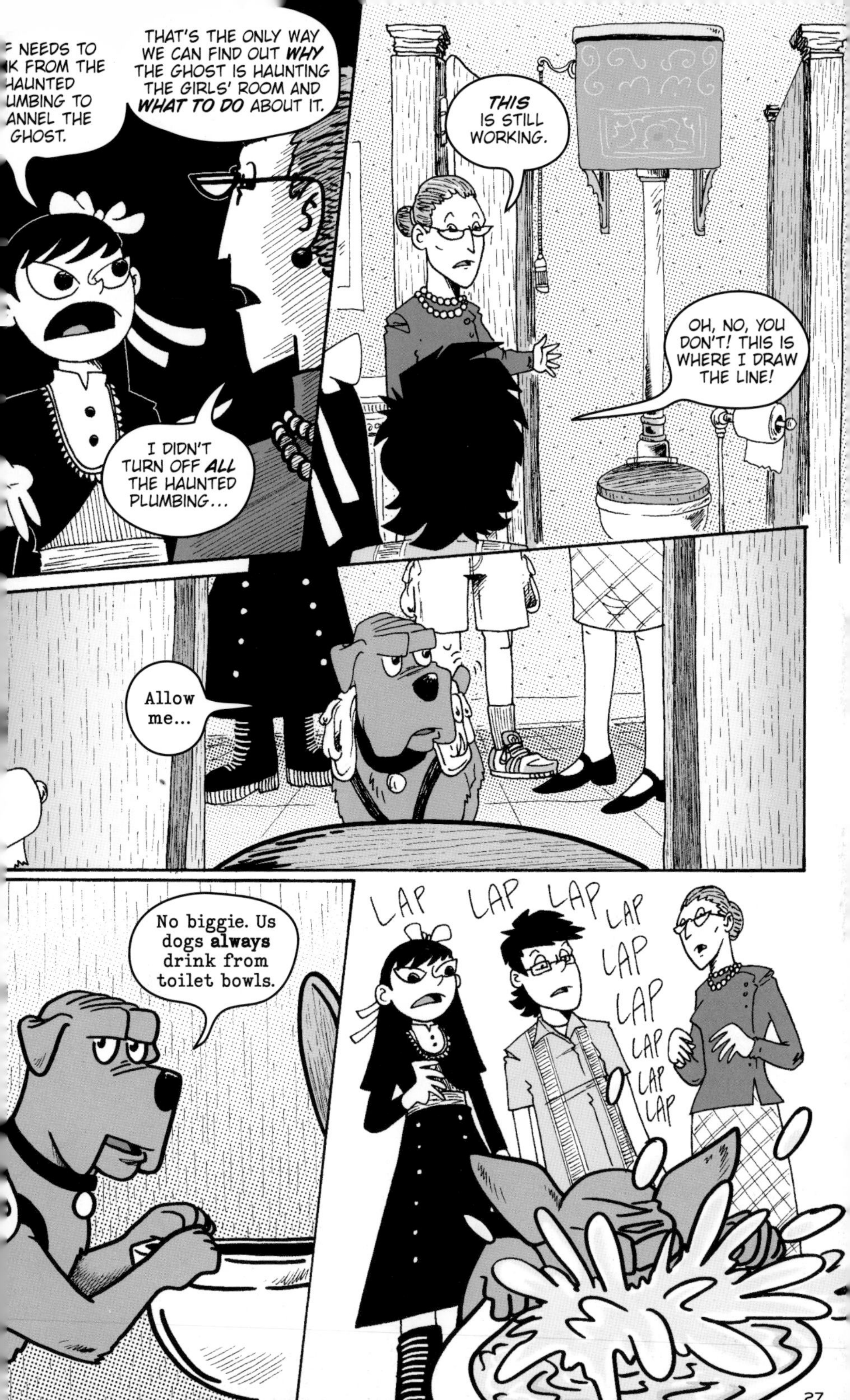
F NEEDS TO
K FROM THE
HAUNTED
UMBING TO
ANNEL THE
GHOST.
THAT'S THE ONLY WAY WE CAN FIND OUT *WHY* THE GHOST IS HAUNTING THE GIRLS' ROOM AND *WHAT TO DO* ABOUT IT.
I DIDN'T TURN OFF *ALL* THE HAUNTED PLUMBING...
THIS IS STILL WORKING.
OH, NO, YOU DON'T! THIS IS WHERE I DRAW THE LINE!
Allow me...
No biggie. Us dogs **always** drink from toilet bowls.
LAP LAP LAP LAP LAP LAP LAP LAP LAP

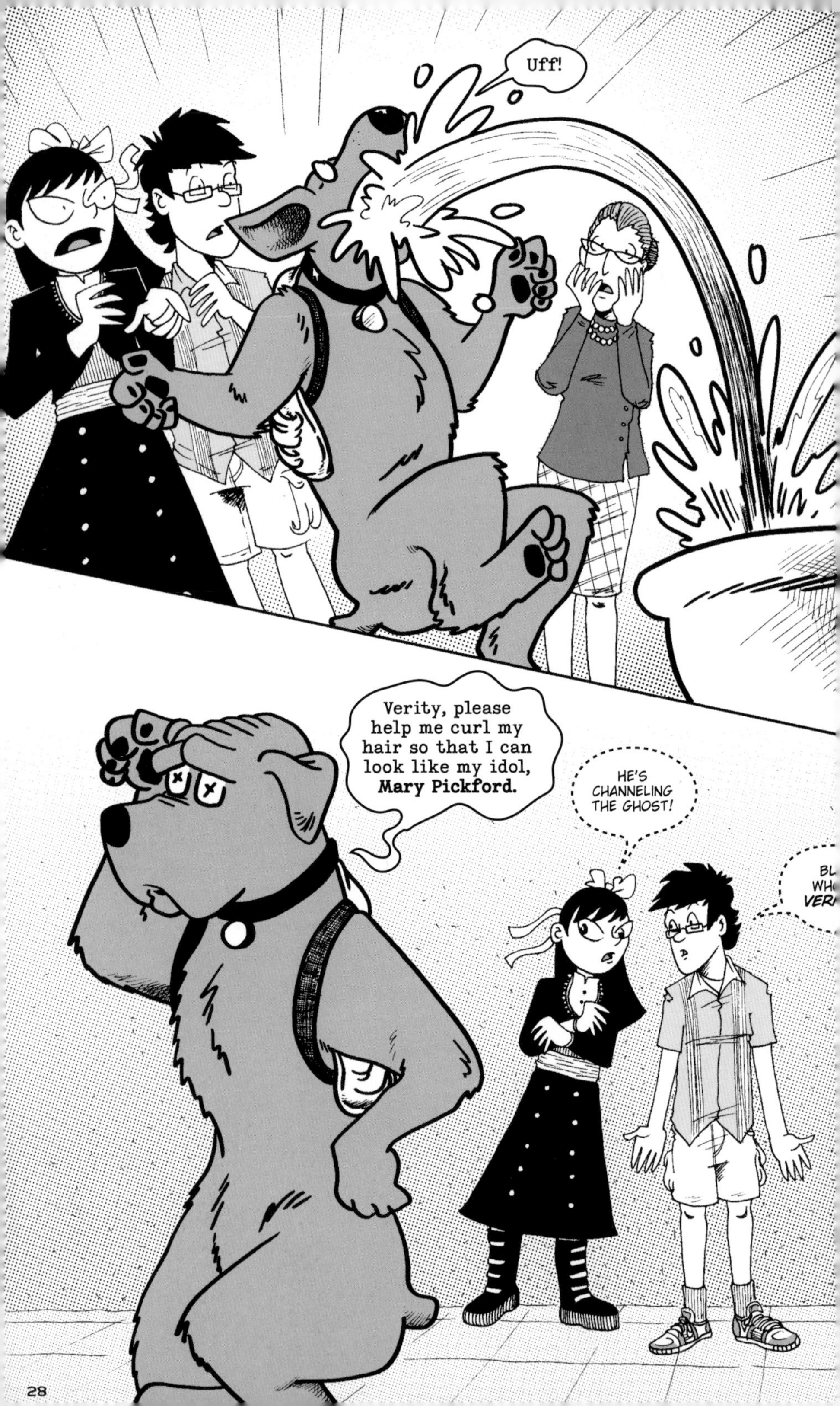
Uff!
Verity, please help me curl my hair so that I can look like my idol, **Mary Pickford.**
HE'S CHANNELING THE GHOST!

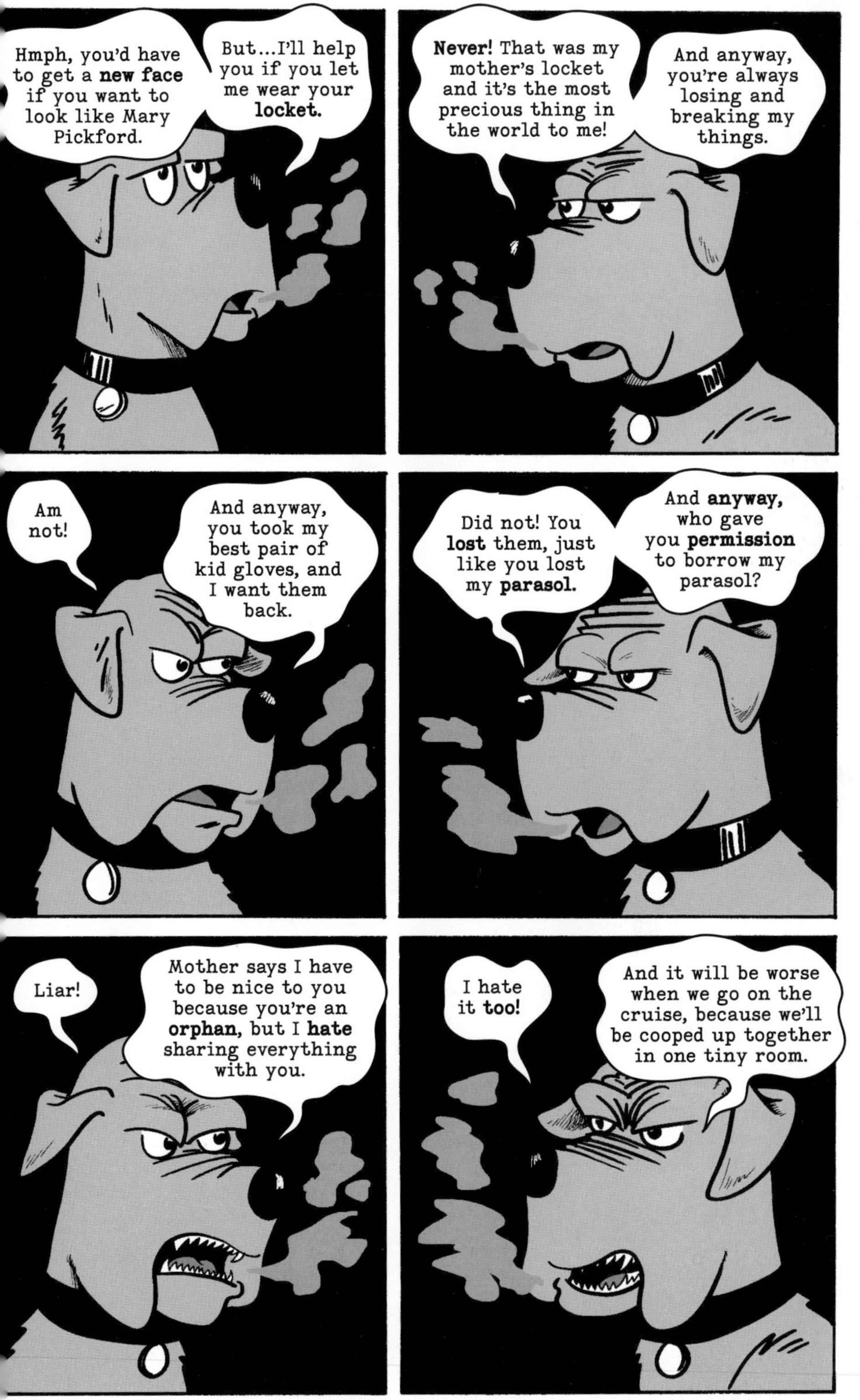
Hmph, you'd have to get a **new face** if you want to look like Mary Pickford.
But...I'll help you if you let me wear your **locket.**
Never! That was my mother's locket and it's the most precious thing in the world to me!
And anyway, you're always losing and breaking my things.
Am not!
And anyway, you took my best pair of kid gloves, and I want them back.
Did not! You **lost** them, just like you lost my **parasol.**
And **anyway,** who gave you **permission** to borrow my parasol?
Liar!
Mother says I have to be nice to you because you're an **orphan,** but I **hate** sharing everything with you.
I hate it **too!**
And it will be worse when we go on the cruise, because we'll be cooped up together in one tiny room.

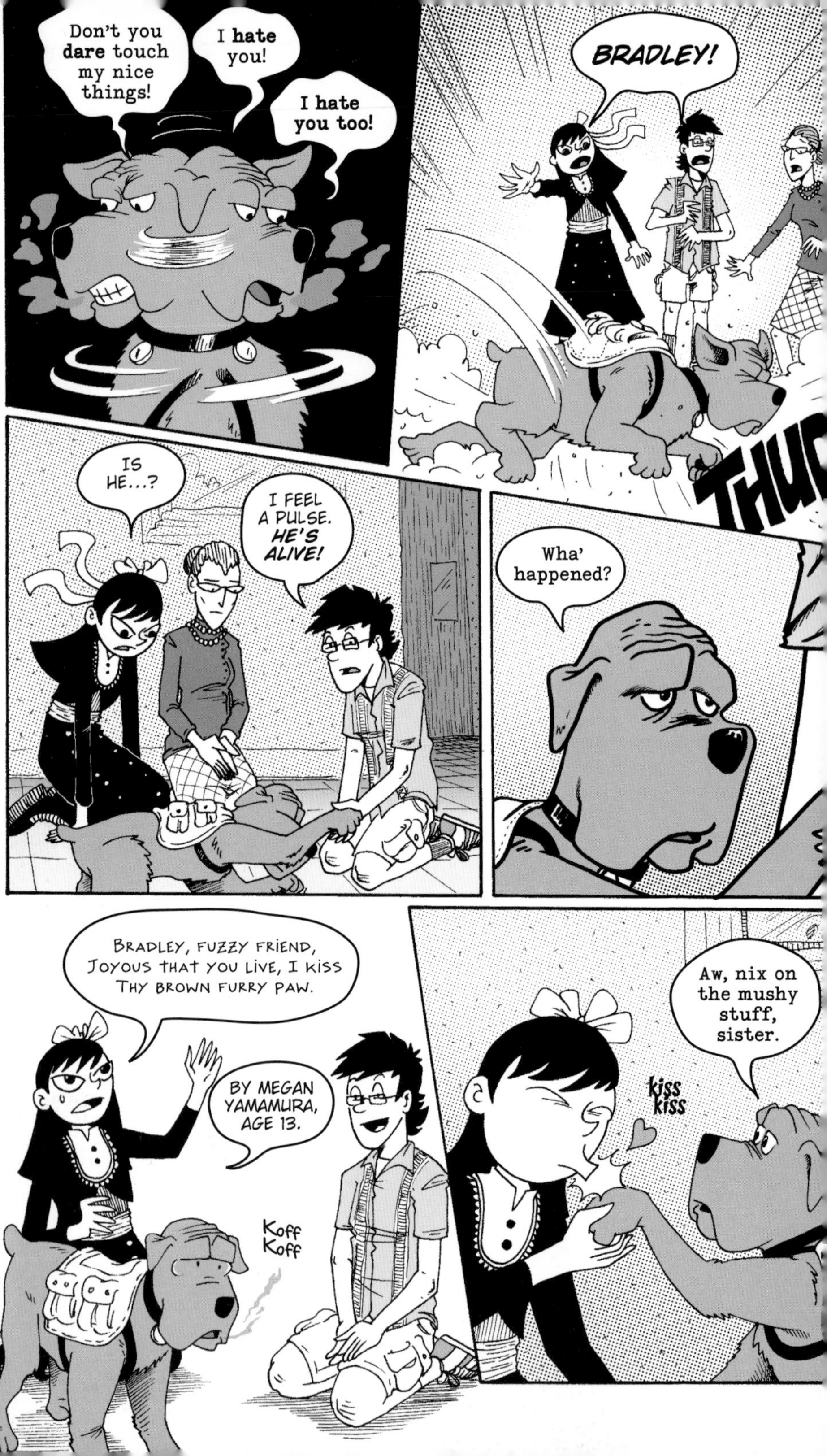

Don't you dare touch my nice things!
I hate you!
I hate you too!
BRADLEY!
THU
IS HE...?
I FEEL A PULSE. HE'S ALIVE!
Wha' happened?
BRADLEY, FUZZY FRIEND, JOYOUS THAT YOU LIVE, I KISS THY BROWN FURRY PAW.
BY MEGAN YAMAMURA, AGE 13.
Koff Koff
Aw, nix on the mushy stuff, sister.
kiss kiss

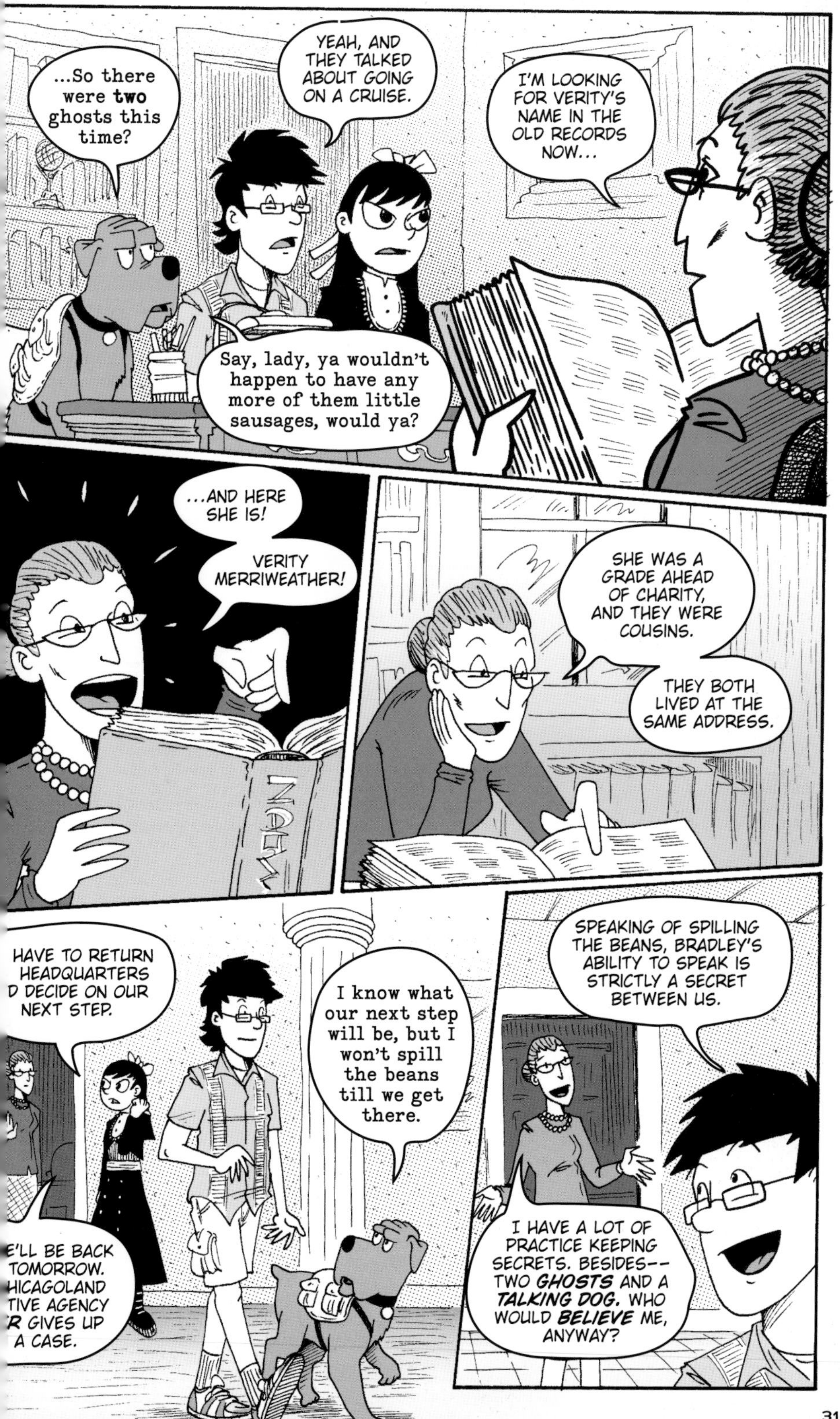

...So there were **two** ghosts this time?
YEAH, AND THEY TALKED ABOUT GOING ON A CRUISE.
I'M LOOKING FOR VERITY'S NAME IN THE OLD RECORDS NOW...
Say, lady, ya wouldn't happen to have any more of them little sausages, would ya?
...AND HERE SHE IS!
VERITY MERRIWEATHER!
SHE WAS A GRADE AHEAD OF CHARITY, AND THEY WERE COUSINS.
THEY BOTH LIVED AT THE SAME ADDRESS.
HAVE TO RETURN HEADQUARTERS D DECIDE ON OUR NEXT STEP.
E'LL BE BACK TOMORROW. HICAGOLAND TIVE AGENCY R GIVES UP A CASE.
I know what our next step will be, but I won't spill the beans till we get there.
SPEAKING OF SPILLING THE BEANS, BRADLEY'S ABILITY TO SPEAK IS STRICTLY A SECRET BETWEEN US.
I HAVE A LOT OF PRACTICE KEEPING SECRETS. BESIDES-- TWO ***GHOSTS*** AND A ***TALKING DOG.*** WHO WOULD ***BELIEVE*** ME, ANYWAY?

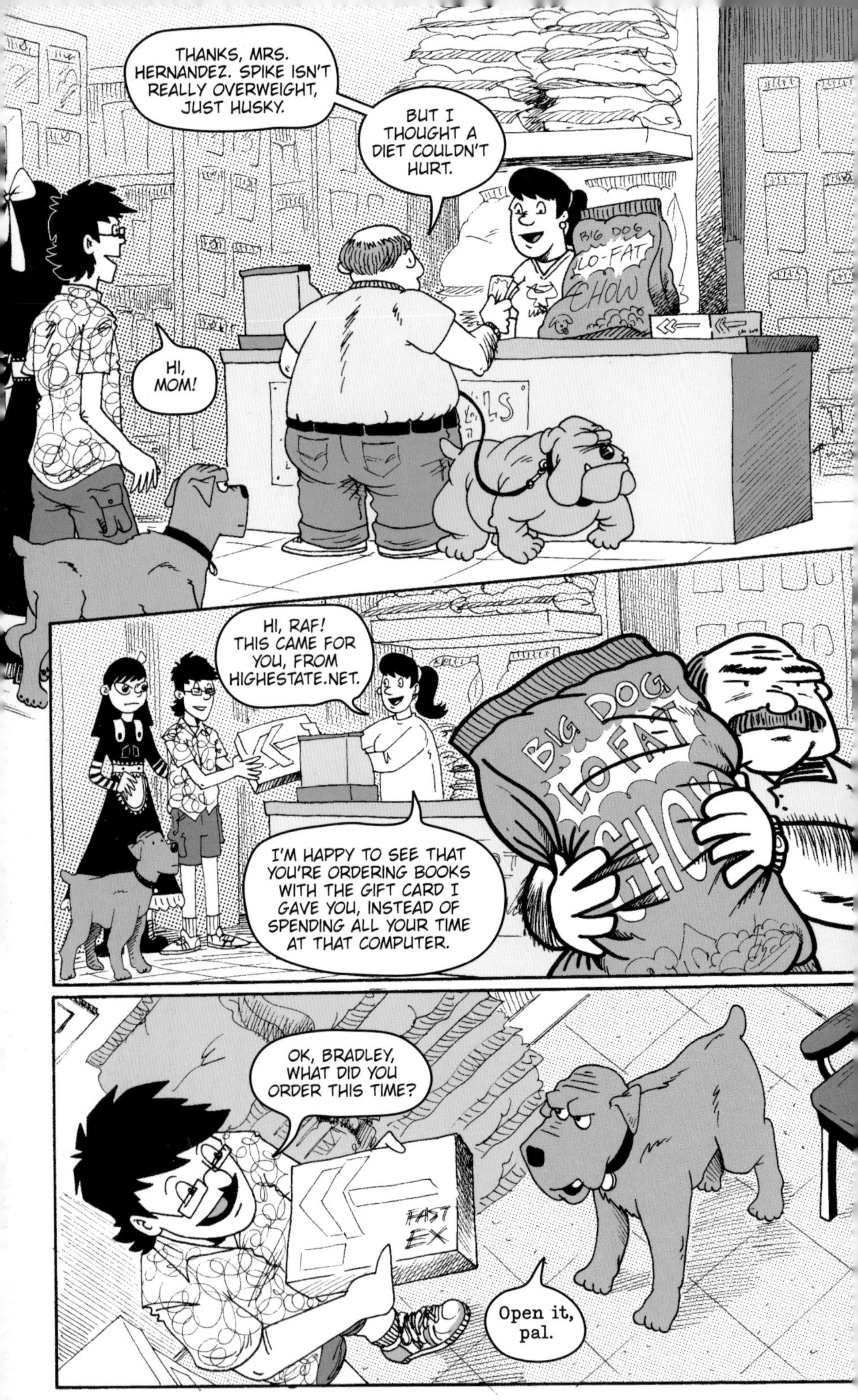
THANKS, MRS. HERNANDEZ. SPIKE ISN'T REALLY OVERWEIGHT, JUST HUSKY.
BUT I THOUGHT A DIET COULDN'T HURT.
BIG DOG LO-FAT CHOW
HI, MOM!
HI, RAF! THIS CAME FOR YOU, FROM HIGHESTATE.NET.
I'M HAPPY TO SEE THAT YOU'RE ORDERING BOOKS WITH THE GIFT CARD I GAVE YOU, INSTEAD OF SPENDING ALL YOUR TIME AT THAT COMPUTER.
BIG DOG LO FAT CHOW
OK, BRADLEY, WHAT DID YOU ORDER THIS TIME?
FAST EX
Open it, pal.

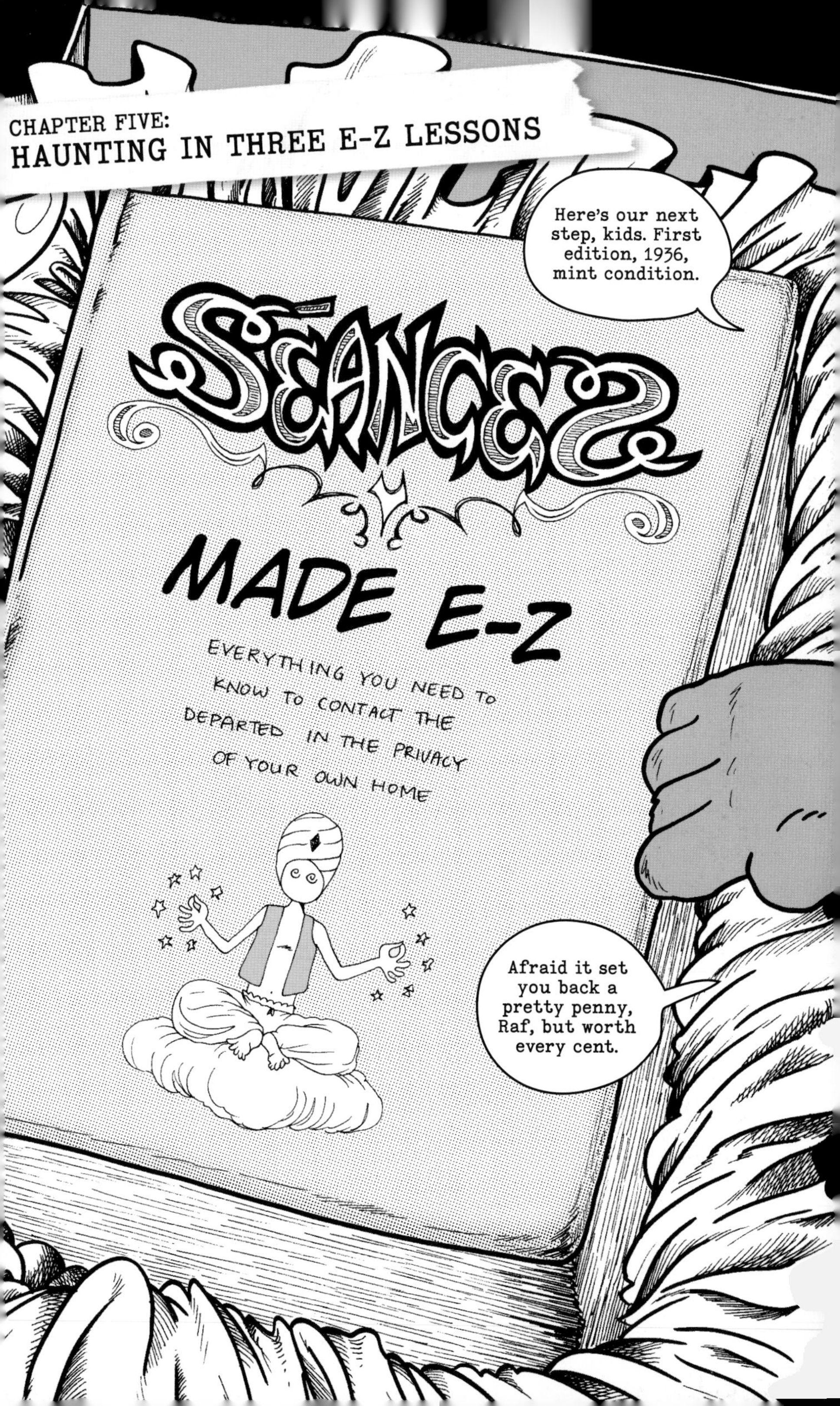
CHAPTER FIVE:
HAUNTING IN THREE E-Z LESSONS
Here's our next step, kids. First edition, 1936, mint condition.
SÉANCES
MADE E-Z
EVERYTHING YOU NEED TO KNOW TO CONTACT THE DEPARTED IN THE PRIVACY OF YOUR OWN HOME
Afraid it set you back a pretty penny, Raf, but worth every cent.

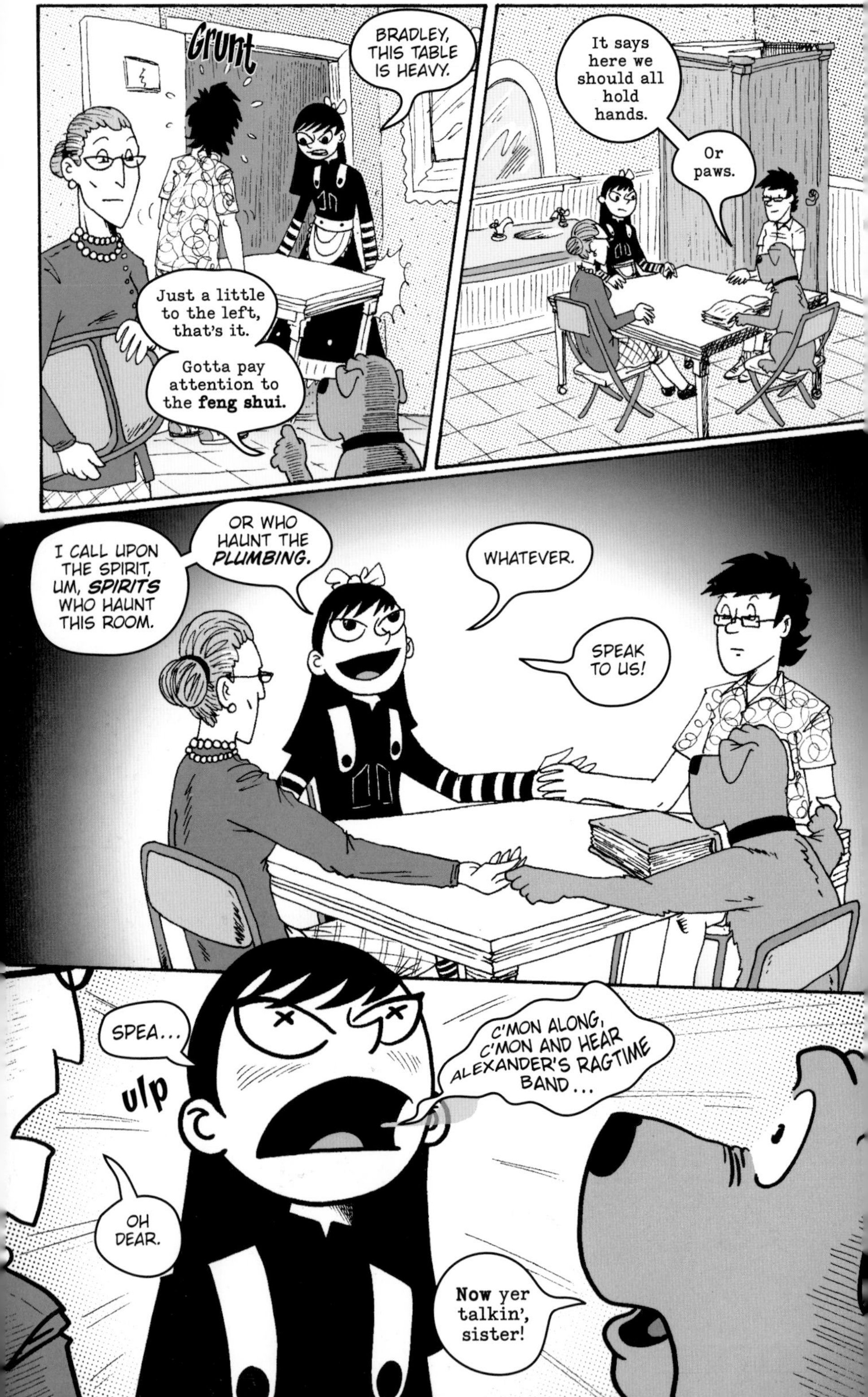

Grunt
BRADLEY, THIS TABLE IS HEAVY.
Just a little to the left, that's it.
Gotta pay attention to the **feng shui.**
It says here we should all hold hands.
Or paws.
I CALL UPON THE SPIRIT, UM, *SPIRITS* WHO HAUNT THIS ROOM.
OR WHO HAUNT THE *PLUMBING.*
WHATEVER.
SPEAK TO US!
SPEA...
ulp
C'MON ALONG, C'MON AND HEAR ALEXANDER'S RAGTIME BAND...
OH DEAR.
Now yer talkin', sister!

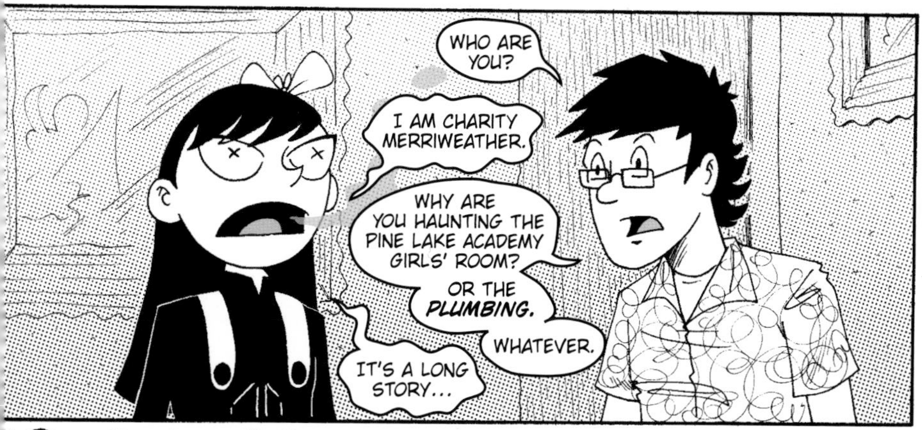
WHO ARE YOU?
I AM CHARITY MERRIWEATHER.
WHY ARE YOU HAUNTING THE PINE LAKE ACADEMY GIRLS' ROOM?
OR THE *PLUMBING.*
WHATEVER.
IT'S A LONG STORY...

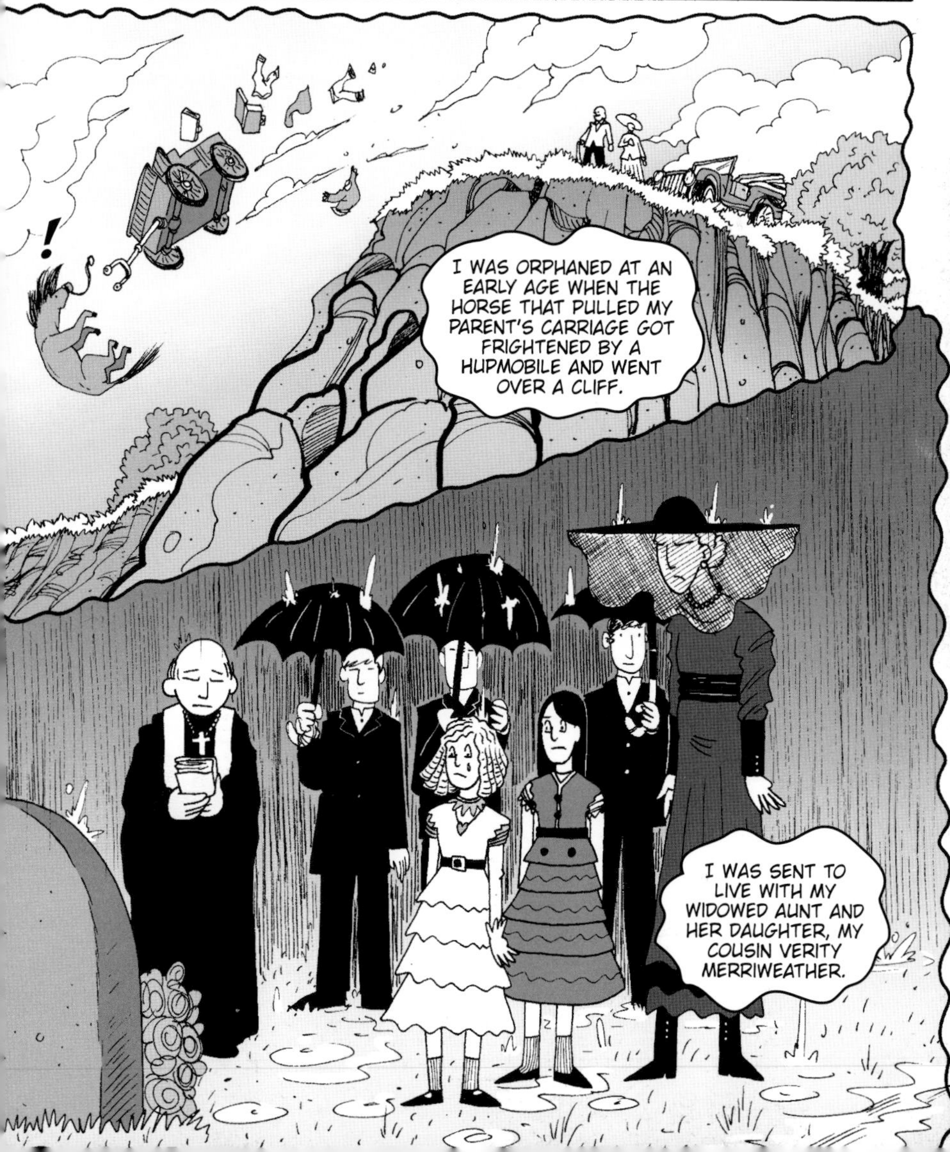
!
I WAS ORPHANED AT AN EARLY AGE WHEN THE HORSE THAT PULLED MY PARENT'S CARRIAGE GOT FRIGHTENED BY A HUPMOBILE AND WENT OVER A CLIFF.
I WAS SENT TO LIVE WITH MY WIDOWED AUNT AND HER DAUGHTER, MY COUSIN VERITY MERRIWEATHER.

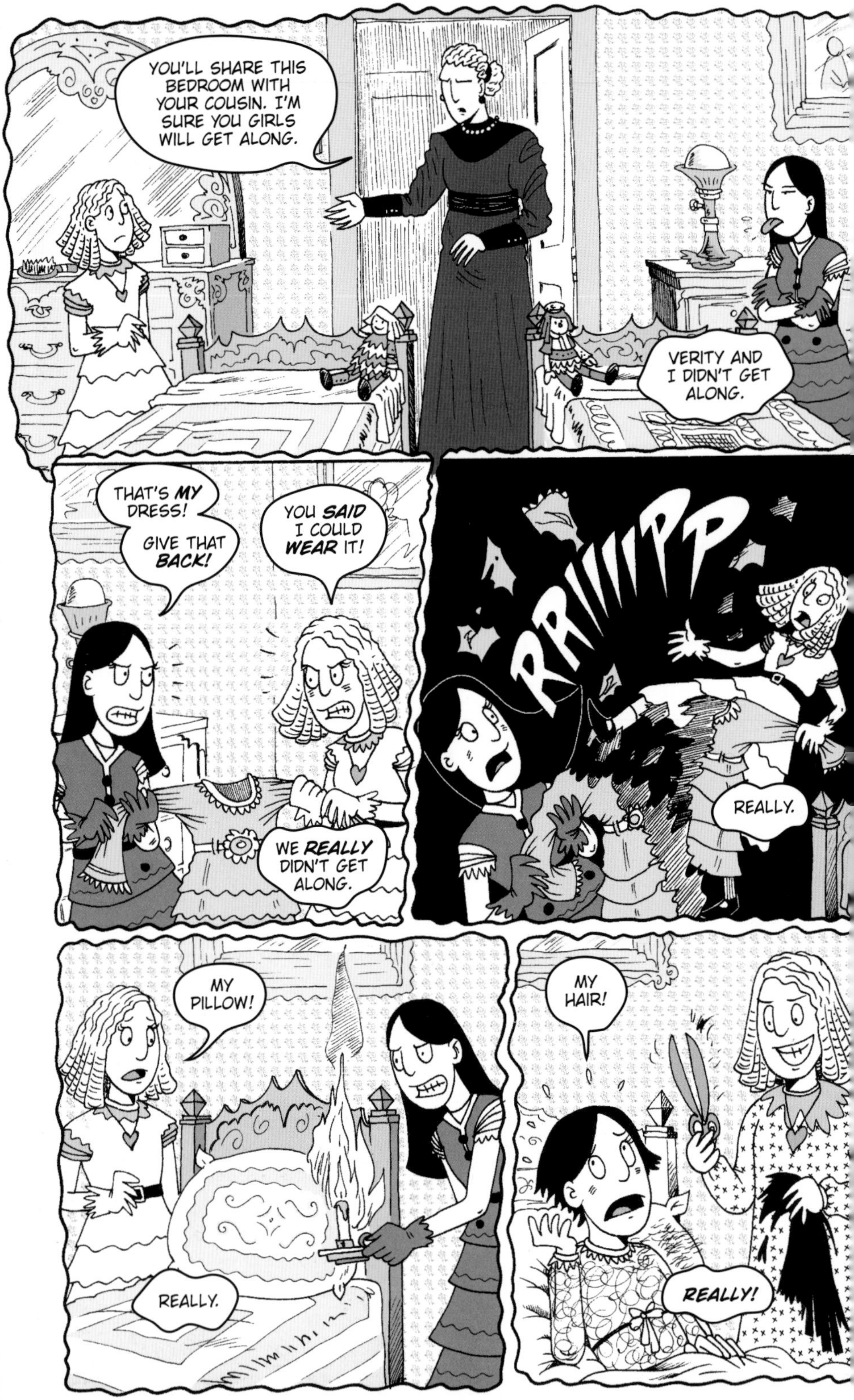
YOU'LL SHARE THIS BEDROOM WITH YOUR COUSIN. I'M SURE YOU GIRLS WILL GET ALONG.
VERITY AND I DIDN'T GET ALONG.
THAT'S MY DRESS!
GIVE THAT BACK!
YOU SAID I COULD WEAR IT!
WE REALLY DIDN'T GET ALONG.
RRIIIIPP
REALLY.
MY PILLOW!
REALLY.
MY HAIR!
REALLY!

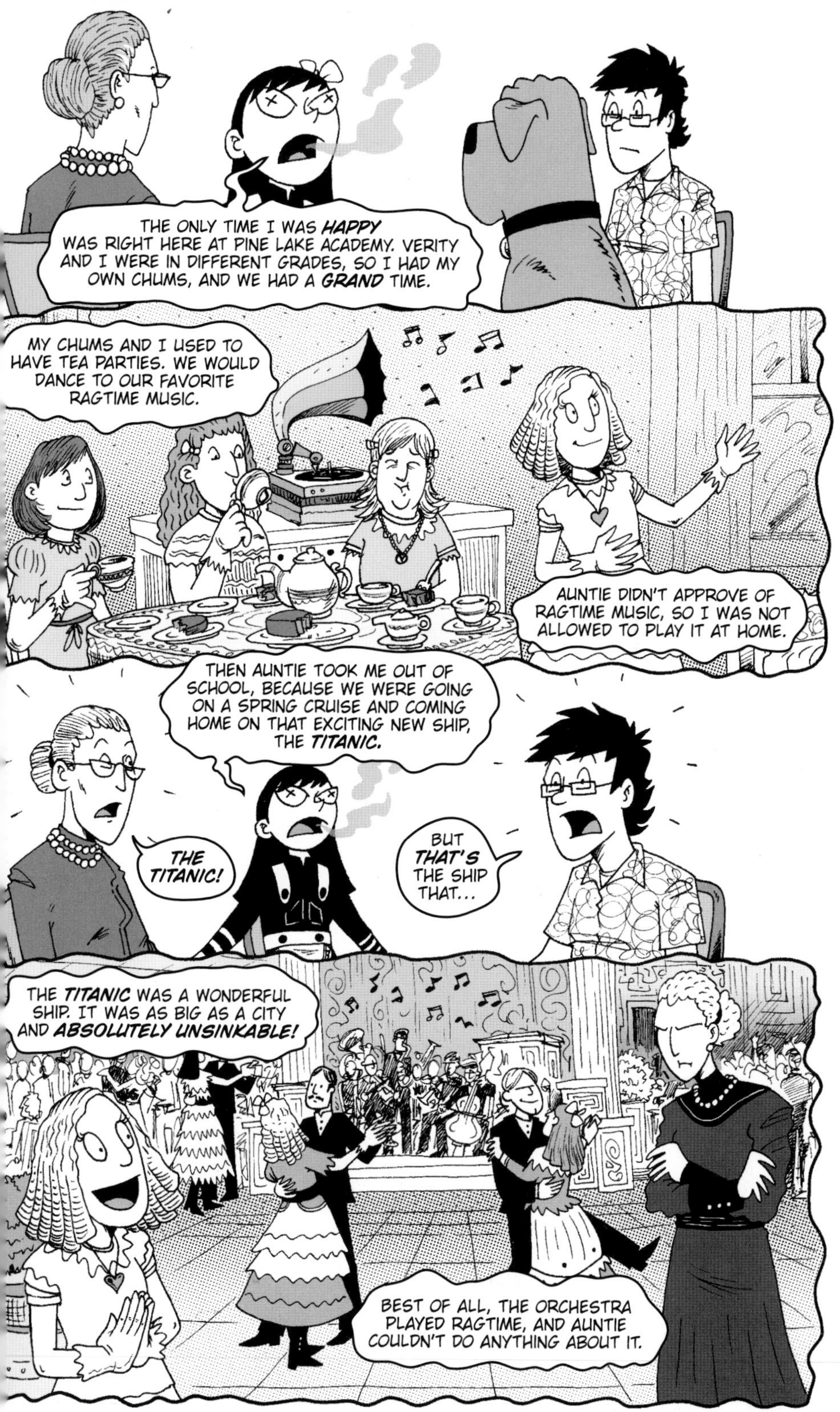

THE ONLY TIME I WAS **HAPPY** WAS RIGHT HERE AT PINE LAKE ACADEMY. VERITY AND I WERE IN DIFFERENT GRADES, SO I HAD MY OWN CHUMS, AND WE HAD A **GRAND** TIME.
MY CHUMS AND I USED TO HAVE TEA PARTIES. WE WOULD DANCE TO OUR FAVORITE RAGTIME MUSIC.
AUNTIE DIDN'T APPROVE OF RAGTIME MUSIC, SO I WAS NOT ALLOWED TO PLAY IT AT HOME.
THEN AUNTIE TOOK ME OUT OF SCHOOL, BECAUSE WE WERE GOING ON A SPRING CRUISE AND COMING HOME ON THAT EXCITING NEW SHIP, THE ***TITANIC.***
THE TITANIC!
BUT ***THAT'S*** THE SHIP THAT...
THE ***TITANIC*** WAS A WONDERFUL SHIP. IT WAS AS BIG AS A CITY AND ***ABSOLUTELY UNSINKABLE!***
BEST OF ALL, THE ORCHESTRA PLAYED RAGTIME, AND AUNTIE COULDN'T DO ANYTHING ABOUT IT.

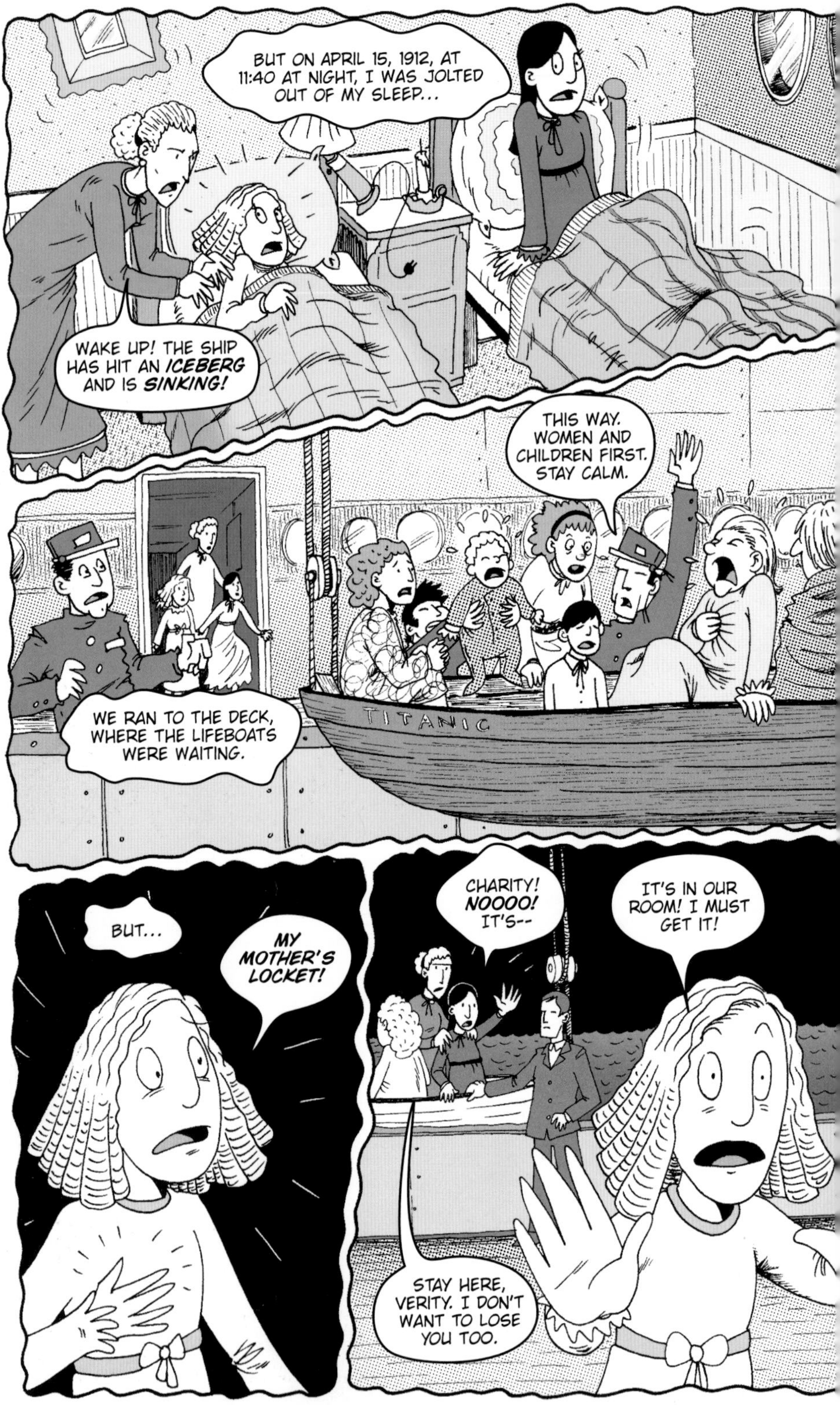
BUT ON APRIL 15, 1912, AT 11:40 AT NIGHT, I WAS JOLTED OUT OF MY SLEEP...
WAKE UP! THE SHIP HAS HIT AN *ICEBERG* AND IS ***SINKING!***
THIS WAY. WOMEN AND CHILDREN FIRST. STAY CALM.
WE RAN TO THE DECK, WHERE THE LIFEBOATS WERE WAITING.
TITANIC
BUT...
MY MOTHER'S LOCKET!
CHARITY! ***NOOOO!*** IT'S--
IT'S IN OUR ROOM! I MUST GET IT!
STAY HERE, VERITY. I DON'T WANT TO LOSE YOU TOO.

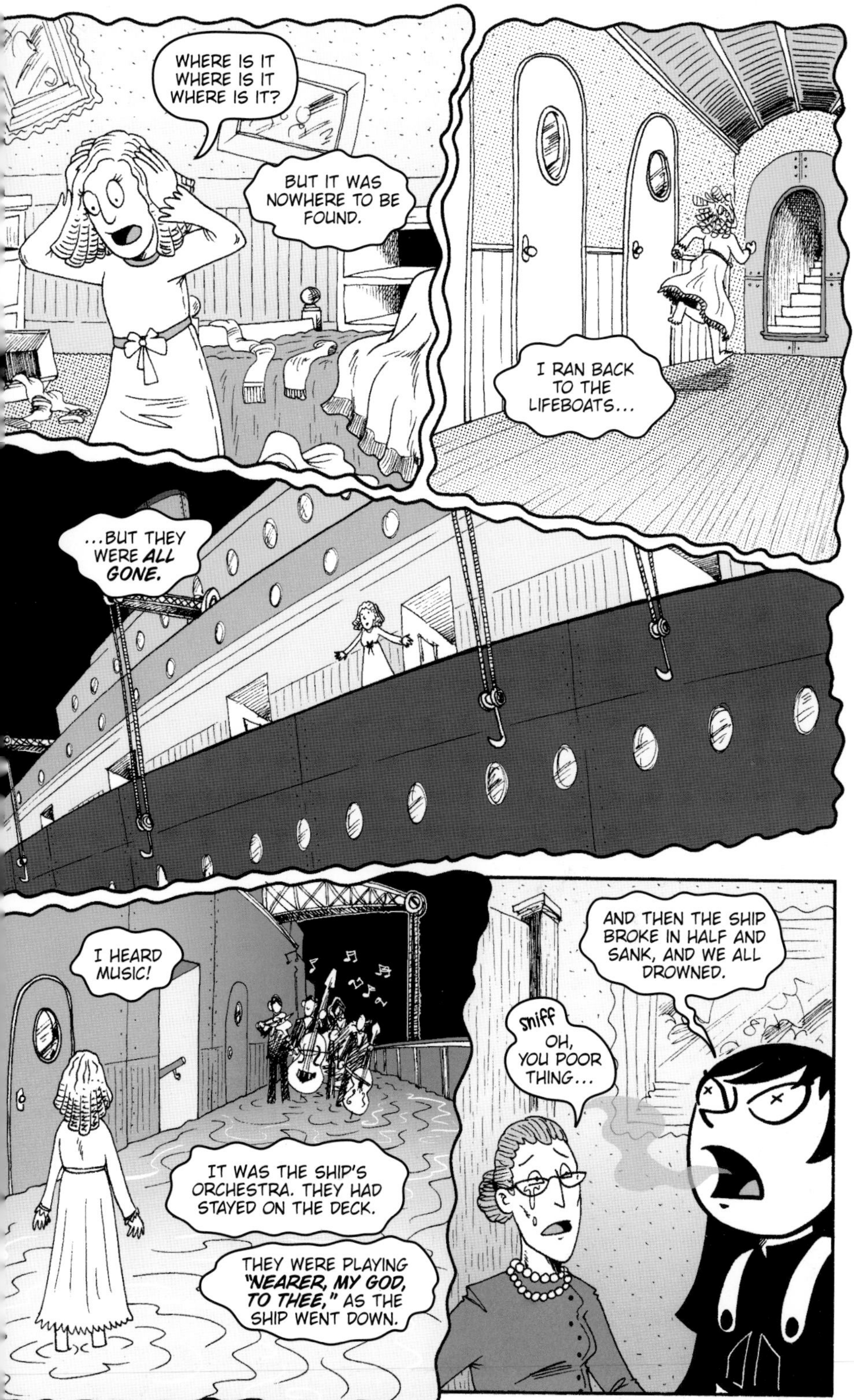

WHERE IS IT WHERE IS IT WHERE IS IT?
BUT IT WAS NOWHERE TO BE FOUND.
I RAN BACK TO THE LIFEBOATS...
...BUT THEY WERE ALL GONE.
I HEARD MUSIC!
IT WAS THE SHIP'S ORCHESTRA. THEY HAD STAYED ON THE DECK.
THEY WERE PLAYING "NEARER, MY GOD, TO THEE," AS THE SHIP WENT DOWN.
AND THEN THE SHIP BROKE IN HALF AND SANK, AND WE ALL DROWNED.
sniff
OH, YOU POOR THING...

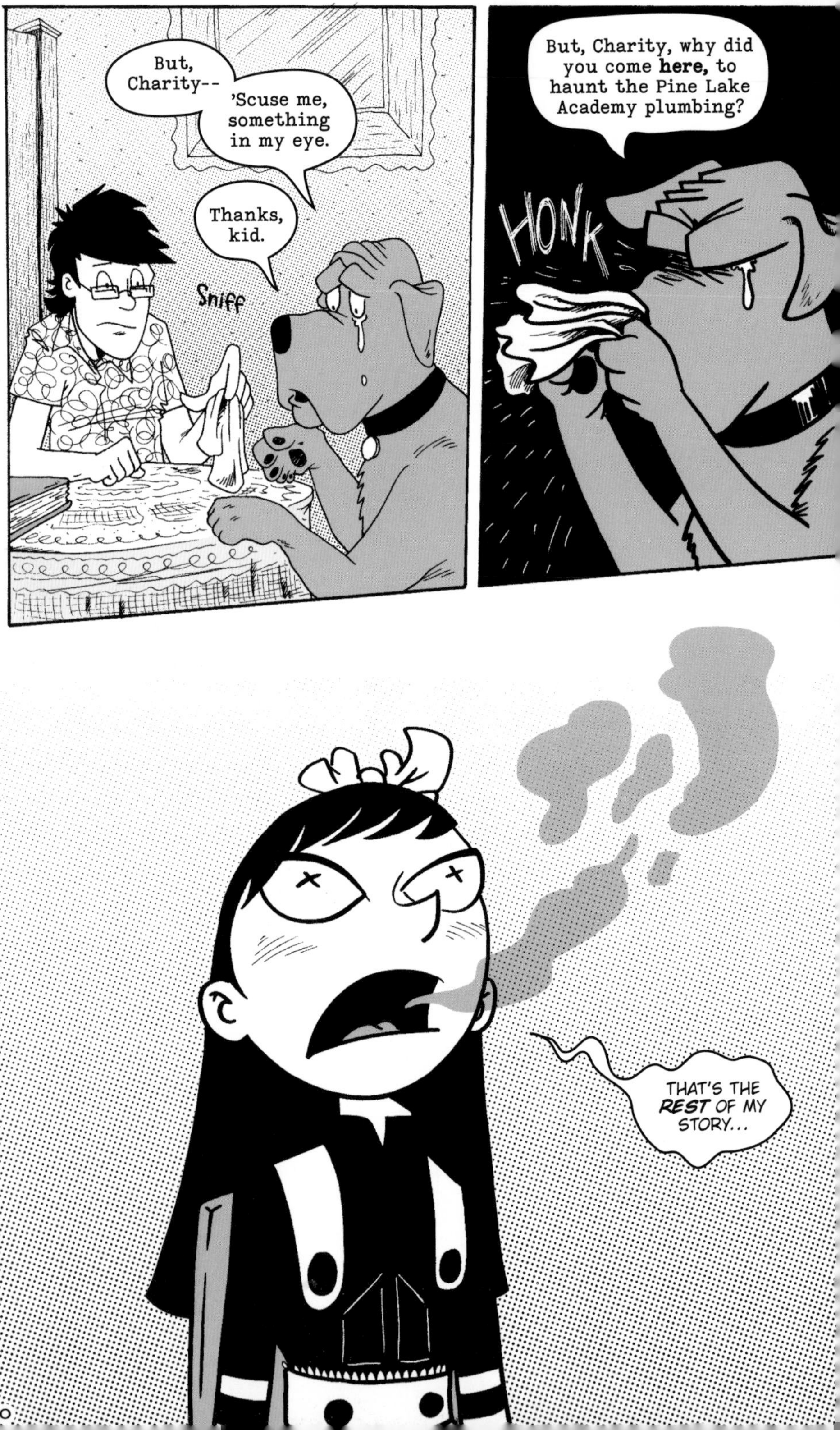
But, Charity--
'Scuse me, something in my eye.
Thanks, kid.
Sniff
But, Charity, why did you come **here,** to haunt the Pine Lake Academy plumbing?
HONK
THAT'S THE ***REST*** OF MY STORY...

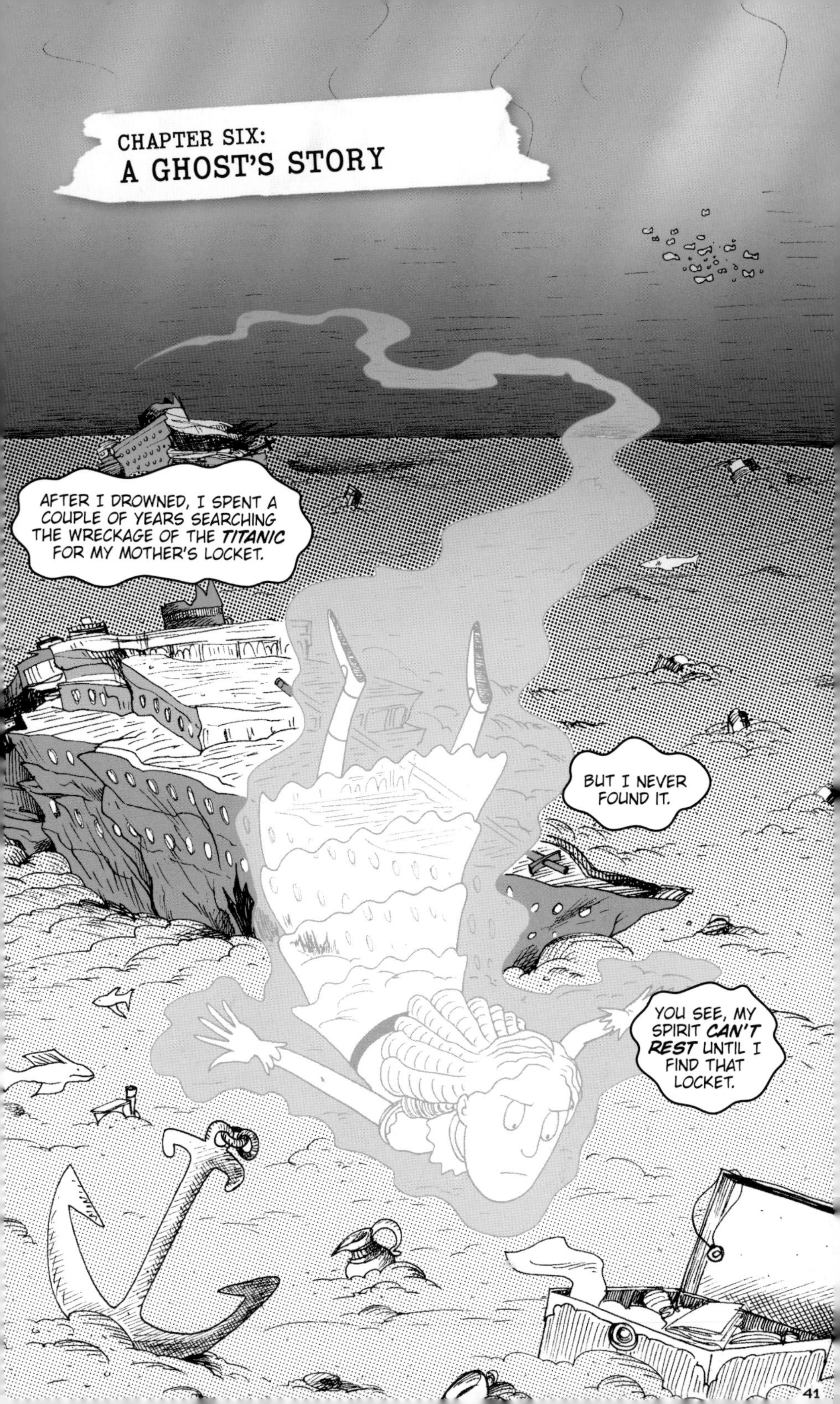
CHAPTER SIX:
A GHOST'S STORY
AFTER I DROWNED, I SPENT A COUPLE OF YEARS SEARCHING THE WRECKAGE OF THE ***TITANIC*** FOR MY MOTHER'S LOCKET.
BUT I NEVER FOUND IT.
YOU SEE, MY SPIRIT ***CAN'T REST*** UNTIL I FIND THAT LOCKET.

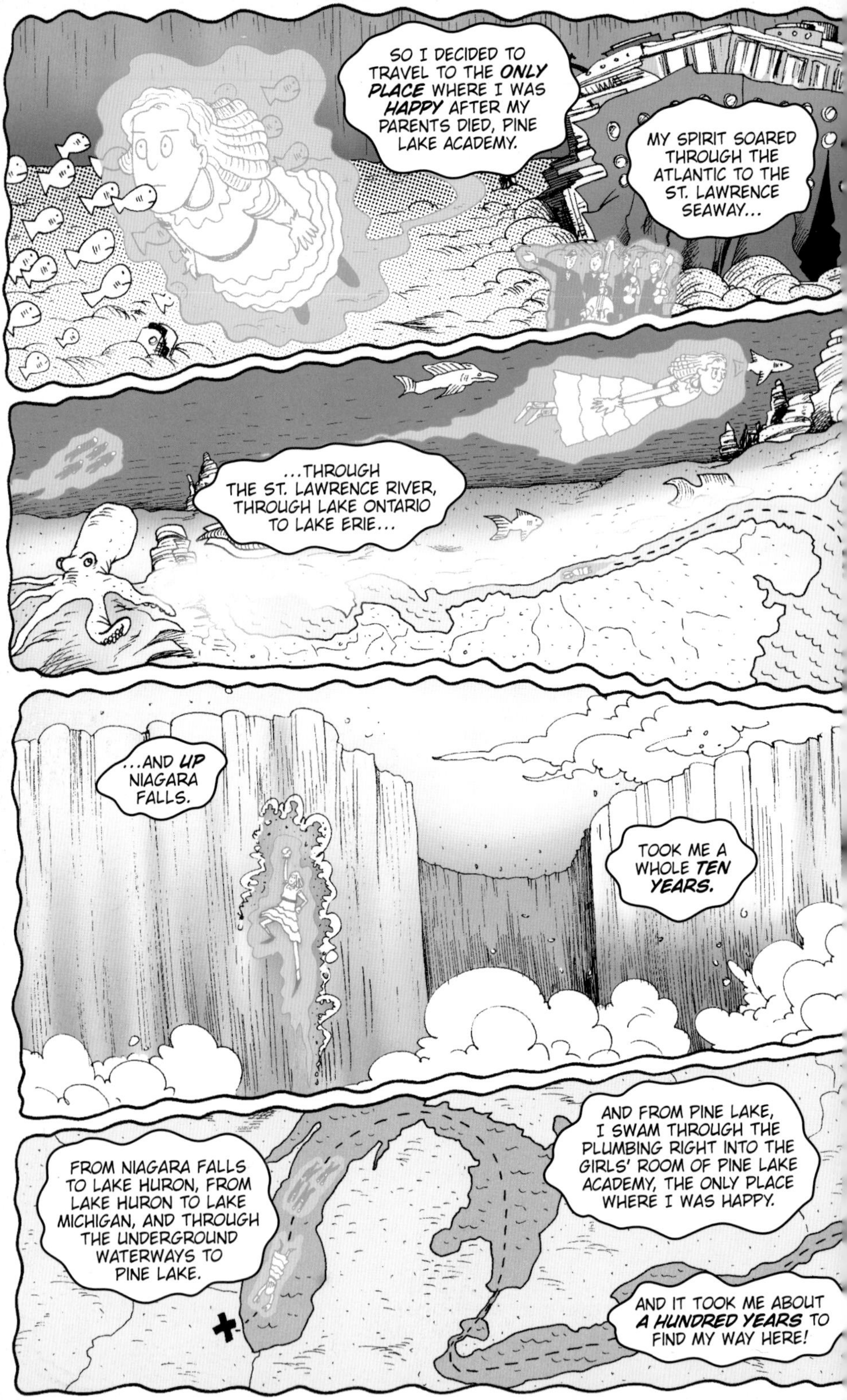
SO I DECIDED TO TRAVEL TO THE ONLY PLACE WHERE I WAS HAPPY AFTER MY PARENTS DIED, PINE LAKE ACADEMY.
MY SPIRIT SOARED THROUGH THE ATLANTIC TO THE ST. LAWRENCE SEAWAY...
...THROUGH THE ST. LAWRENCE RIVER, THROUGH LAKE ONTARIO TO LAKE ERIE...
...AND UP NIAGARA FALLS.
TOOK ME A WHOLE TEN YEARS.
FROM NIAGARA FALLS TO LAKE HURON, FROM LAKE HURON TO LAKE MICHIGAN, AND THROUGH THE UNDERGROUND WATERWAYS TO PINE LAKE.
AND FROM PINE LAKE, I SWAM THROUGH THE PLUMBING RIGHT INTO THE GIRLS' ROOM OF PINE LAKE ACADEMY, THE ONLY PLACE WHERE I WAS HAPPY.
AND IT TOOK ME ABOUT A HUNDRED YEARS TO FIND MY WAY HERE!

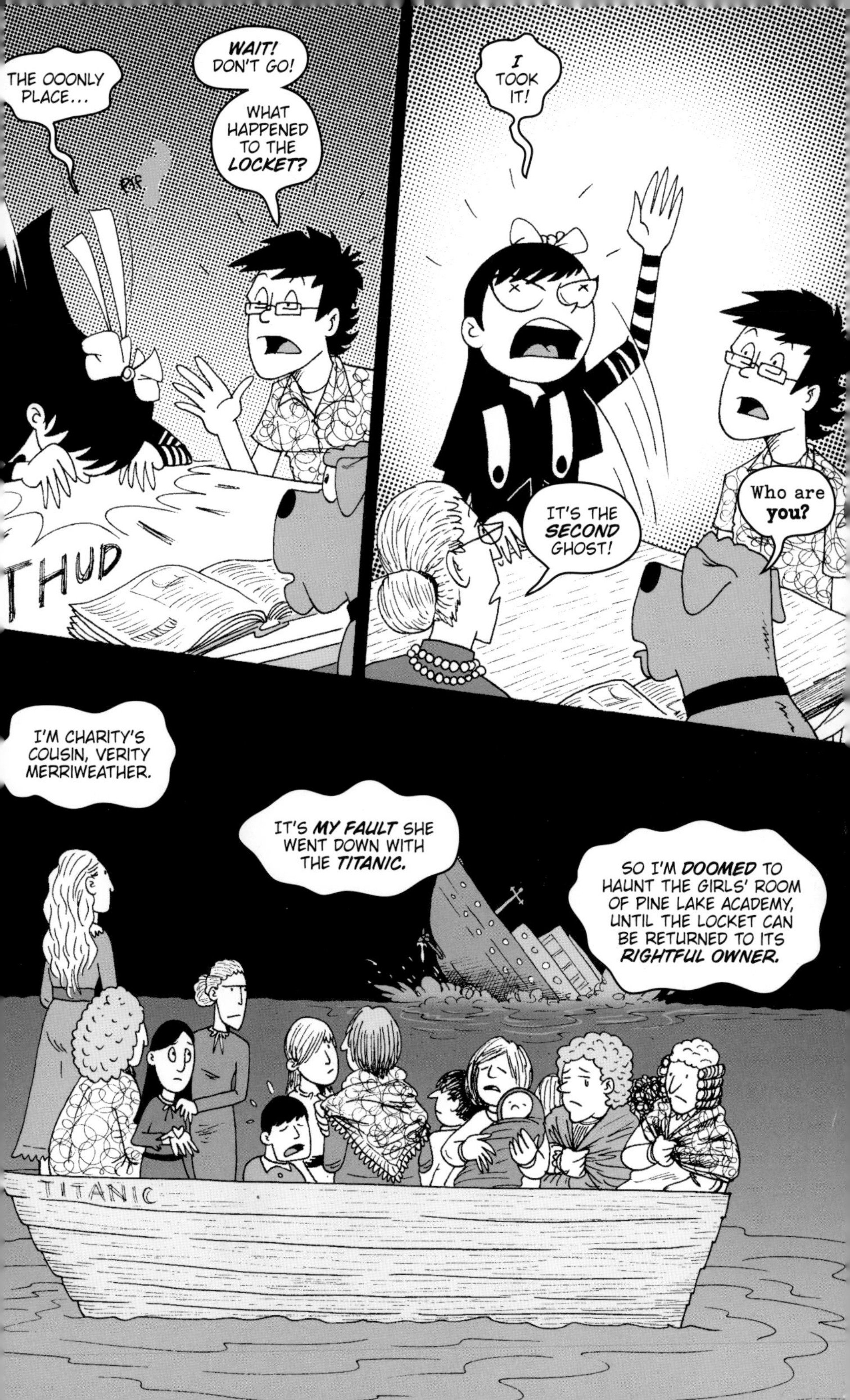
THE OOONLY PLACE...
WAIT! DON'T GO!
WHAT HAPPENED TO THE LOCKET?
THUD
I TOOK IT!
IT'S THE SECOND GHOST!
Who are you?
I'M CHARITY'S COUSIN, VERITY MERRIWEATHER.
IT'S MY FAULT SHE WENT DOWN WITH THE TITANIC.
SO I'M DOOMED TO HAUNT THE GIRLS' ROOM OF PINE LAKE ACADEMY, UNTIL THE LOCKET CAN BE RETURNED TO ITS RIGHTFUL OWNER.
TITANIC

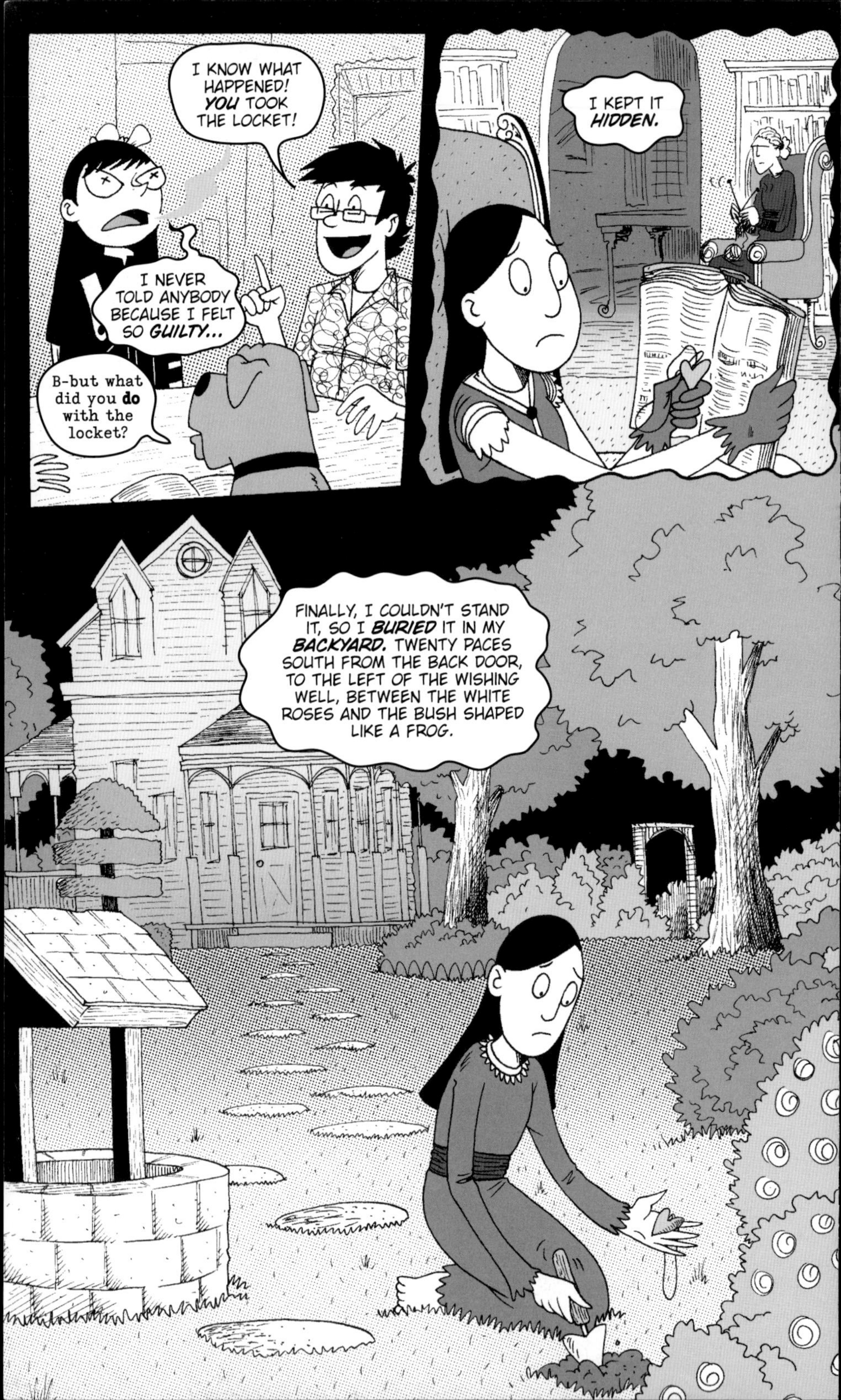
I KNOW WHAT HAPPENED! ***YOU*** TOOK THE LOCKET!
I NEVER TOLD ANYBODY BECAUSE I FELT SO ***GUILTY...***
B-but what did you **do** with the locket?
I KEPT IT ***HIDDEN.***
FINALLY, I COULDN'T STAND IT, SO I ***BURIED*** IT IN MY ***BACKYARD.*** TWENTY PACES SOUTH FROM THE BACK DOOR, TO THE LEFT OF THE WISHING WELL, BETWEEN THE WHITE ROSES AND THE BUSH SHAPED LIKE A FROG.

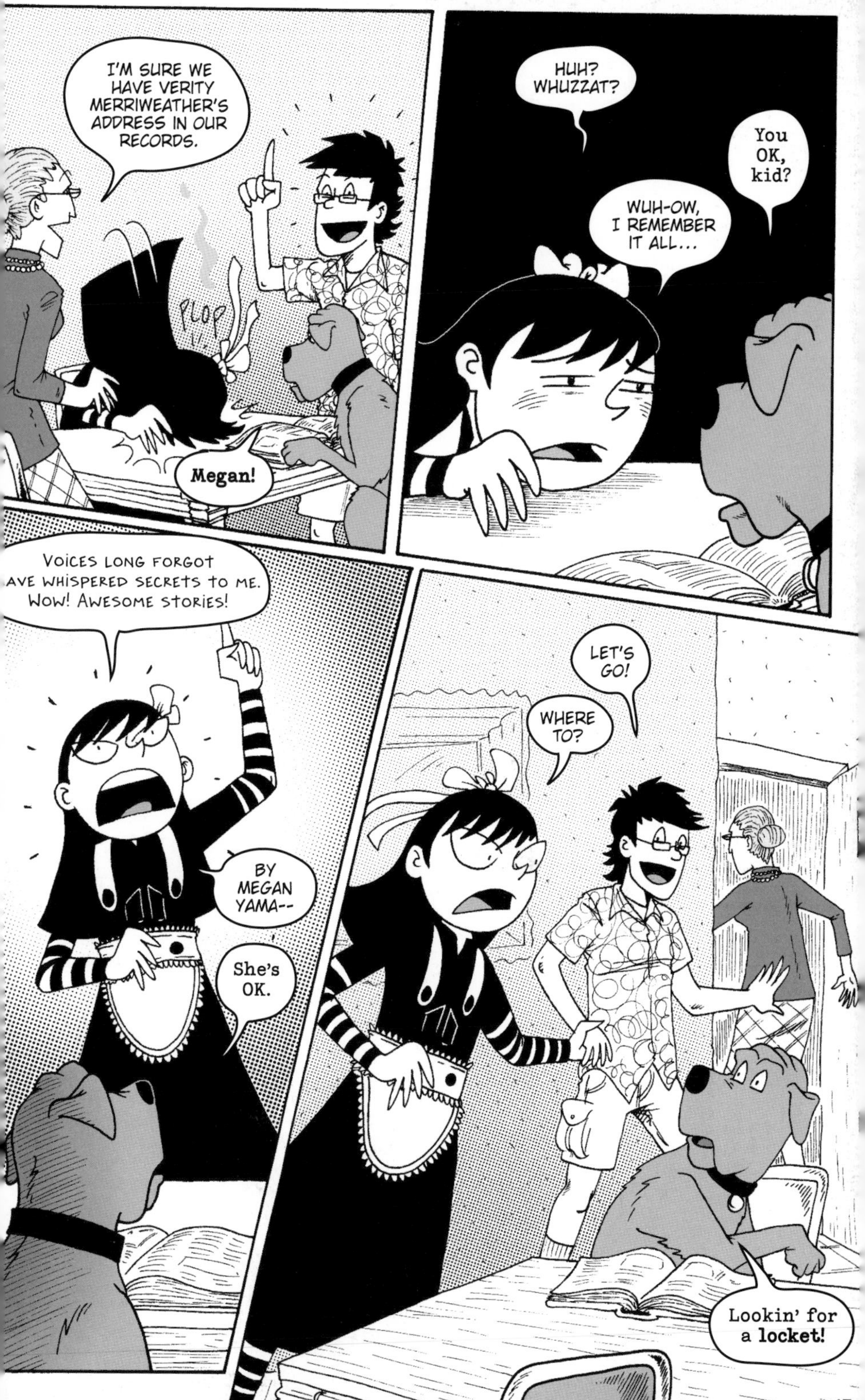
I'M SURE WE HAVE VERITY MERRIWEATHER'S ADDRESS IN OUR RECORDS.
PLOP
Megan!
HUH? WHUZZAT?
WUH-OW, I REMEMBER IT ALL...
You OK, kid?
VOICES LONG FORGOT
AVE WHISPERED SECRETS TO ME.
WOW! AWESOME STORIES!
BY MEGAN YAMA--
She's OK.
LET'S GO!
WHERE TO?
Lookin' for a locket!

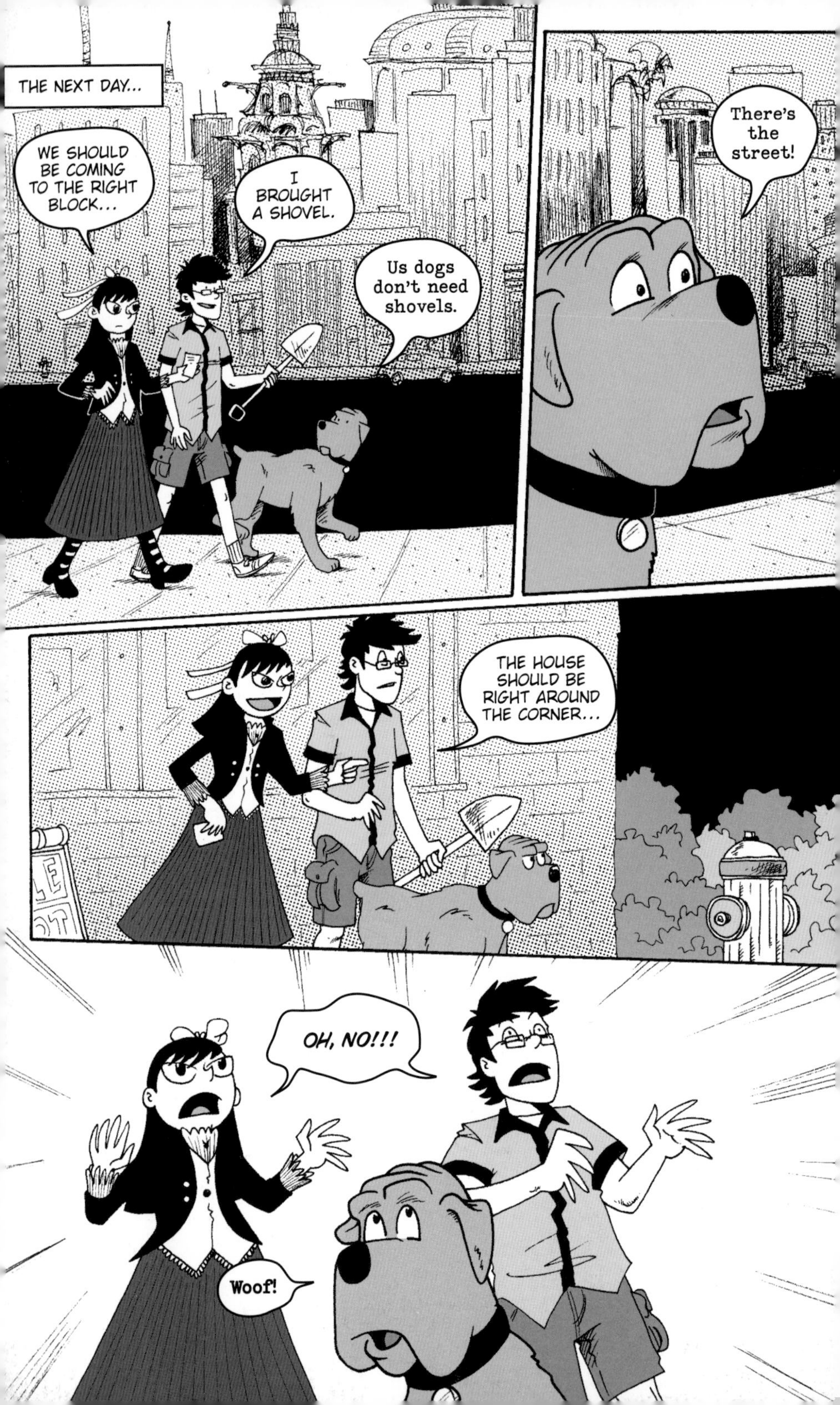
THE NEXT DAY...
WE SHOULD BE COMING TO THE RIGHT BLOCK...
I BROUGHT A SHOVEL.
Us dogs don't need shovels.
There's the street!
THE HOUSE SHOULD BE RIGHT AROUND THE CORNER...
OH, NO!!!
Woof!

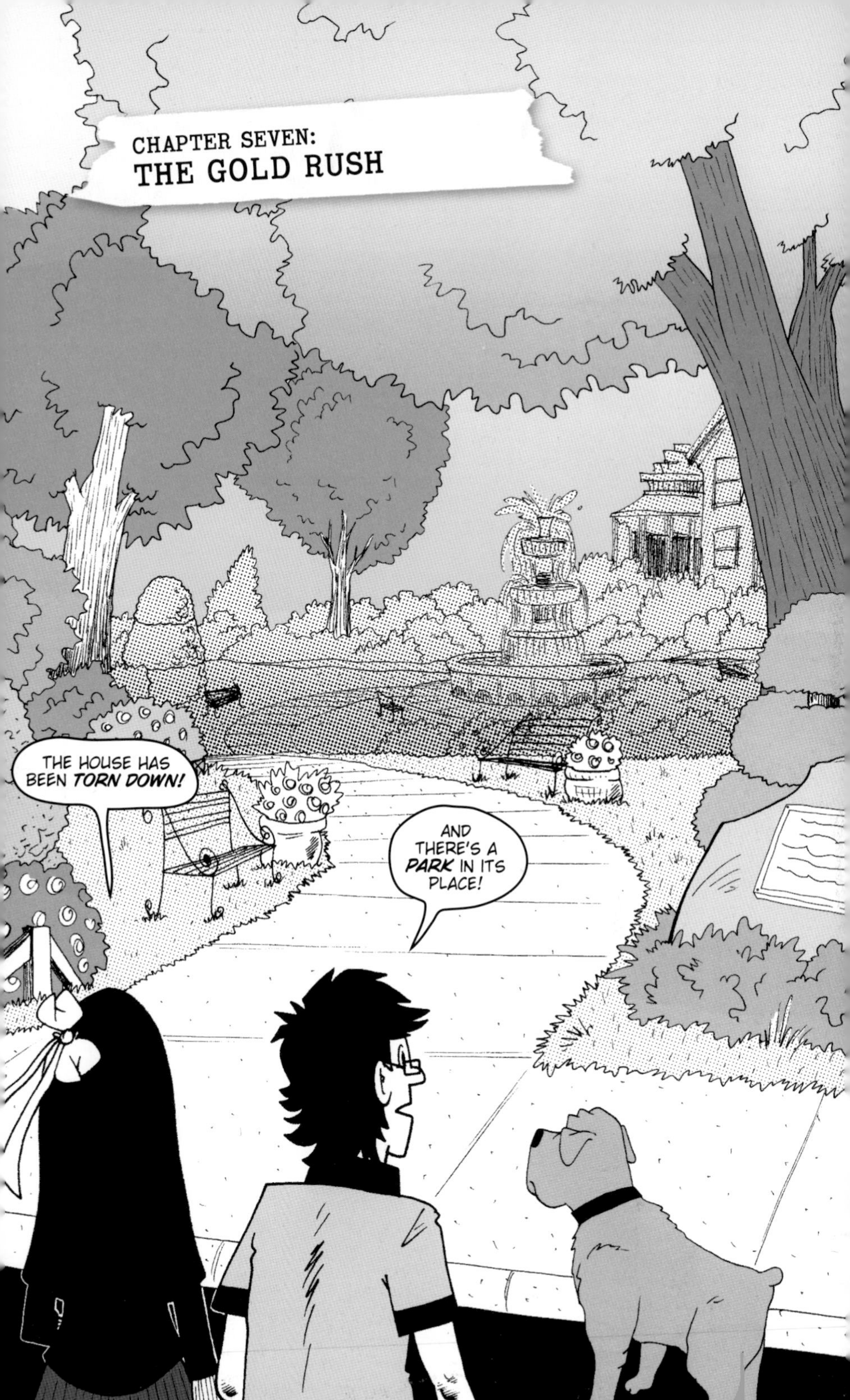
CHAPTER SEVEN:
THE GOLD RUSH
THE HOUSE HAS BEEN TORN DOWN!
AND THERE'S A PARK IN ITS PLACE!

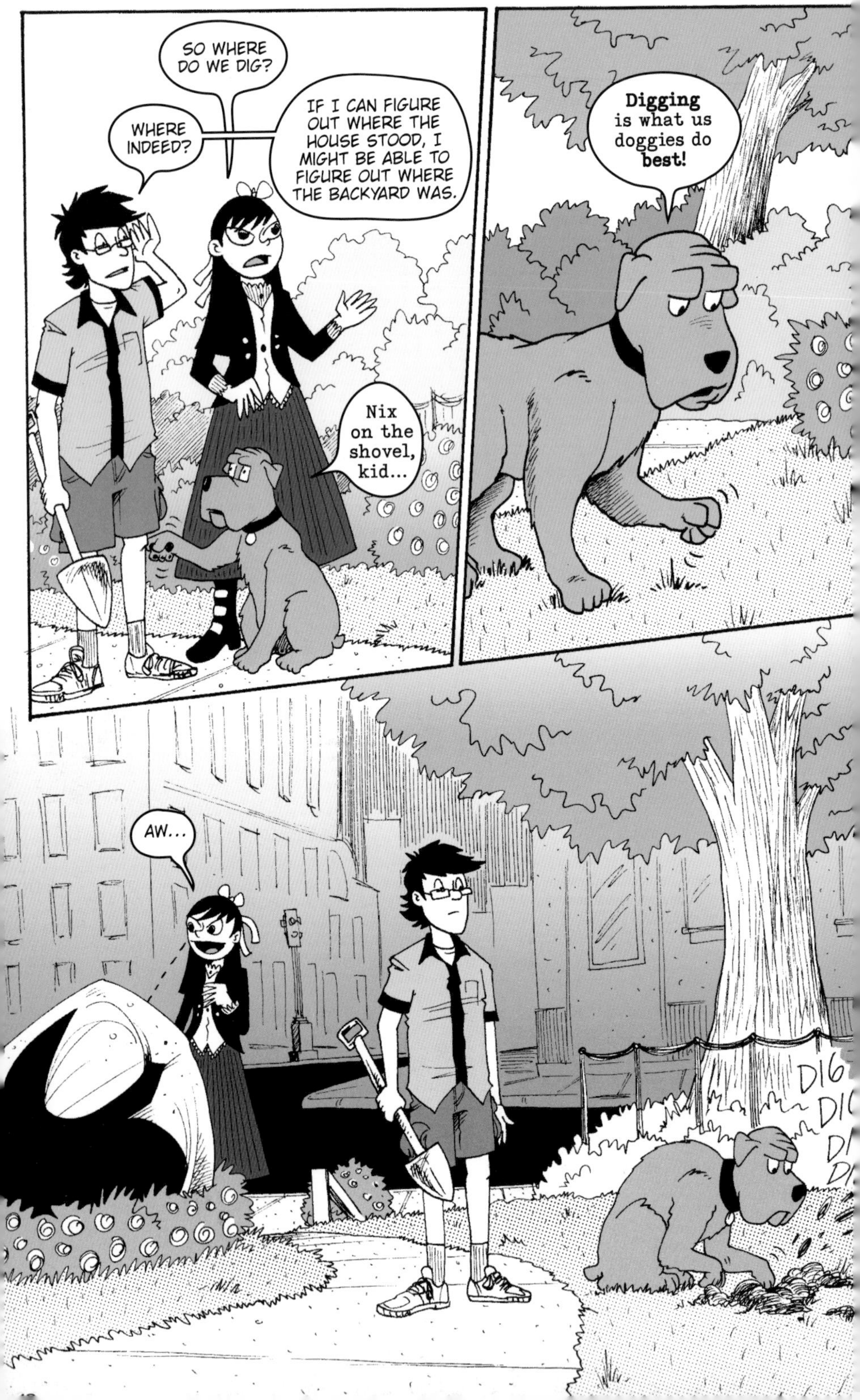
SO WHERE DO WE DIG?
WHERE INDEED?
IF I CAN FIGURE OUT WHERE THE HOUSE STOOD, I MIGHT BE ABLE TO FIGURE OUT WHERE THE BACKYARD WAS.
Nix on the shovel, kid...
Digging is what us doggies do **best!**
AW...

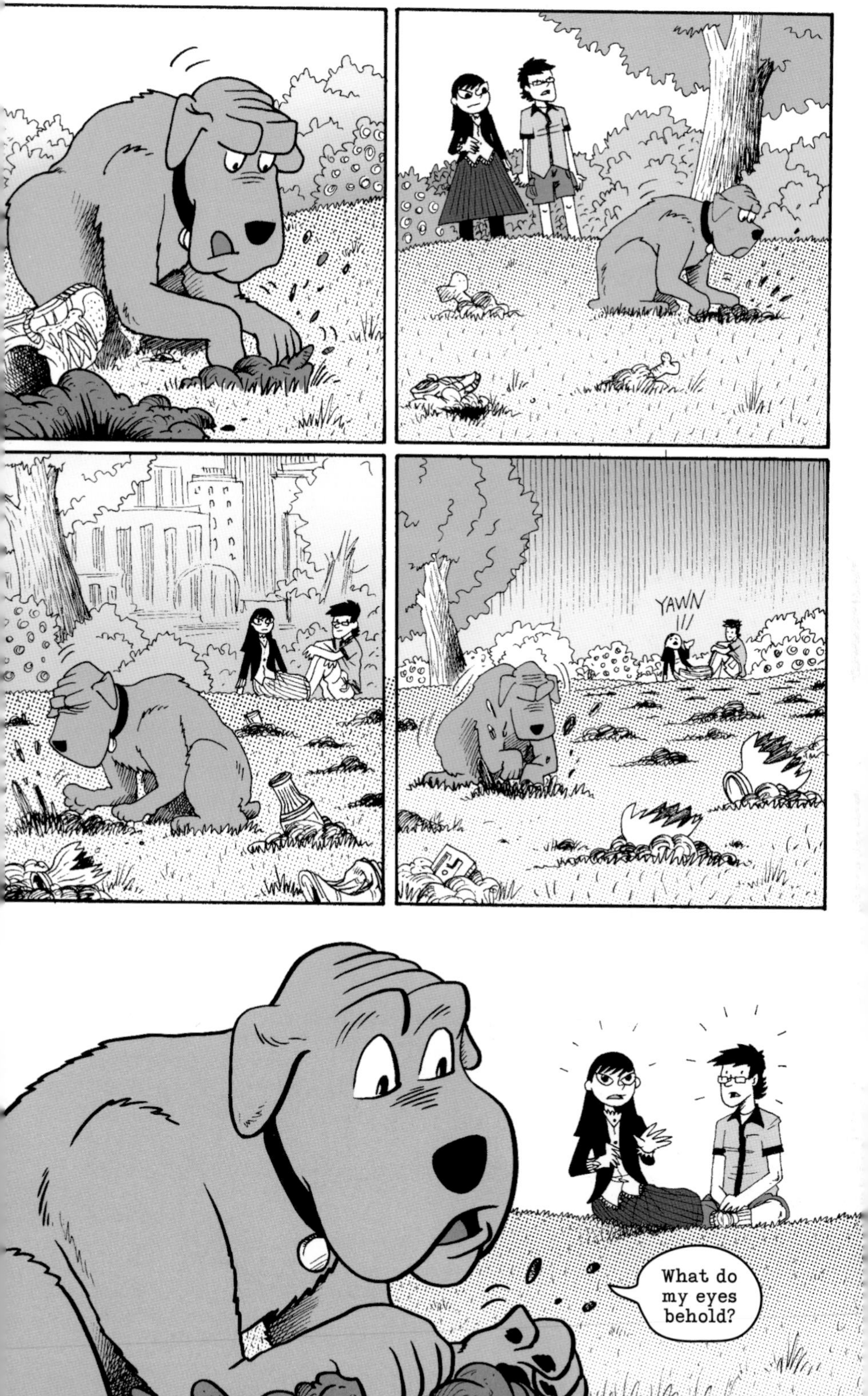
YAWN
What do my eyes behold?

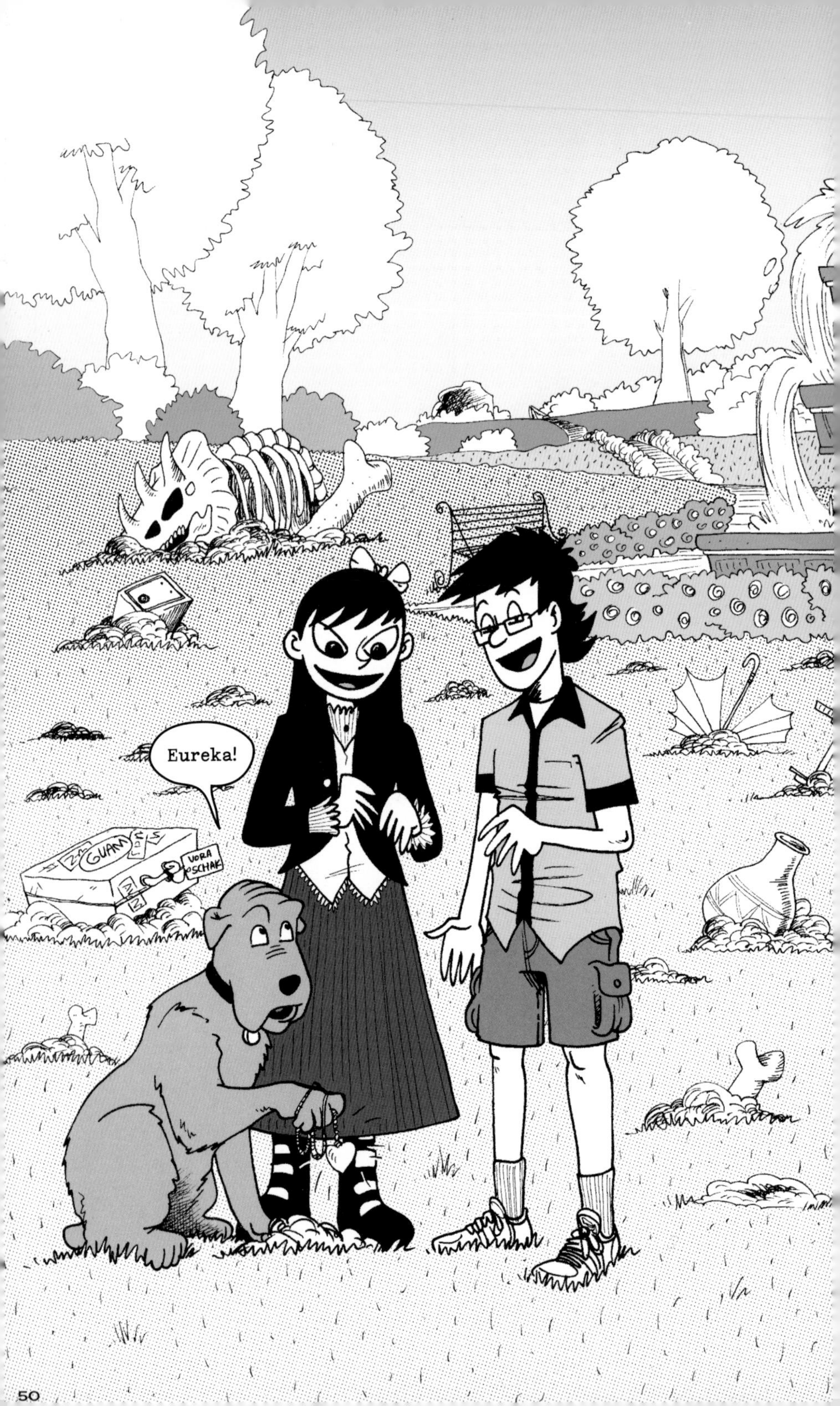
Eureka!
GUAM

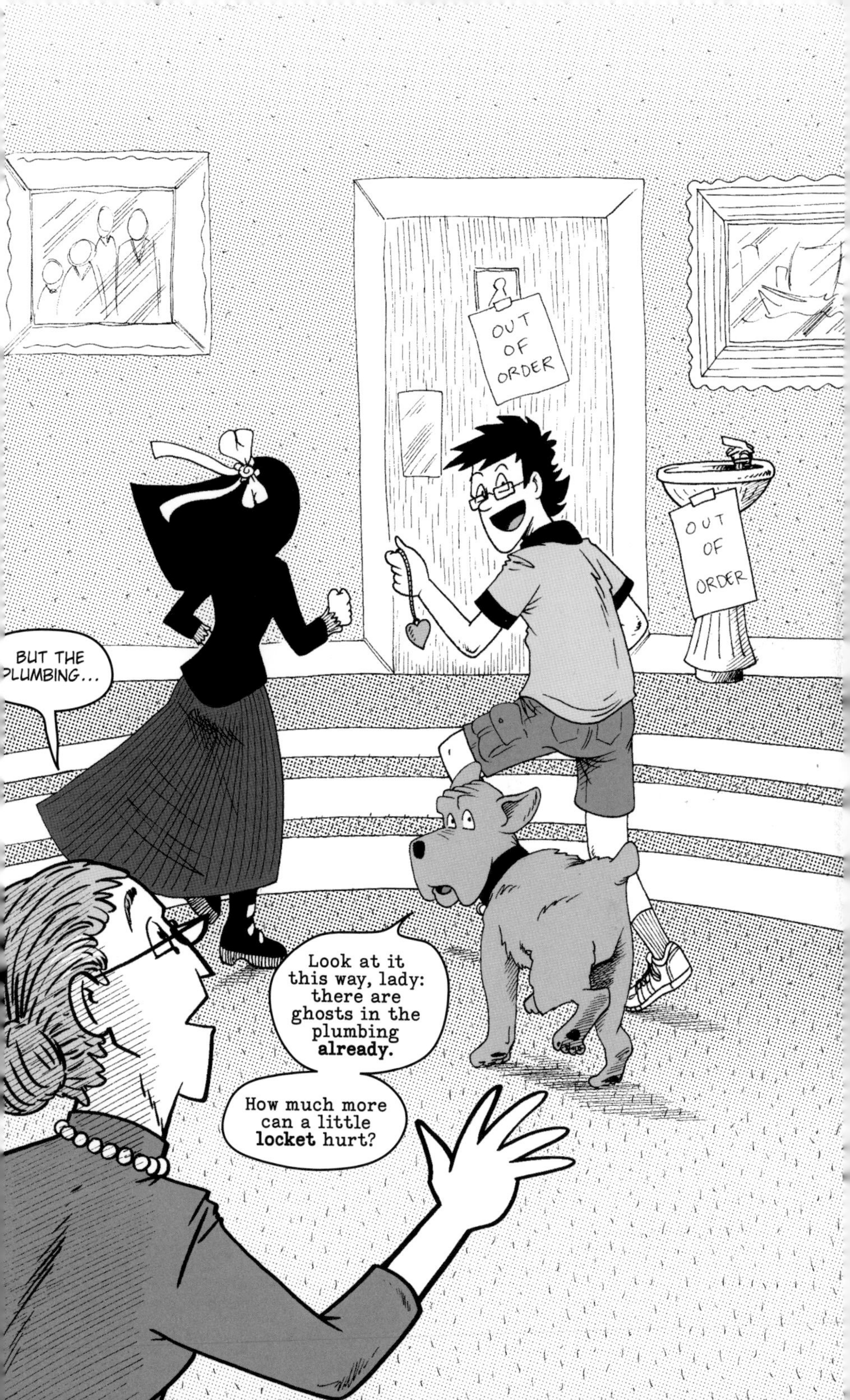
OUT OF ORDER
OUT OF ORDER
BUT THE PLUMBING...
Look at it this way, lady: there are ghosts in the plumbing **already.**
How much more can a little **locket** hurt?

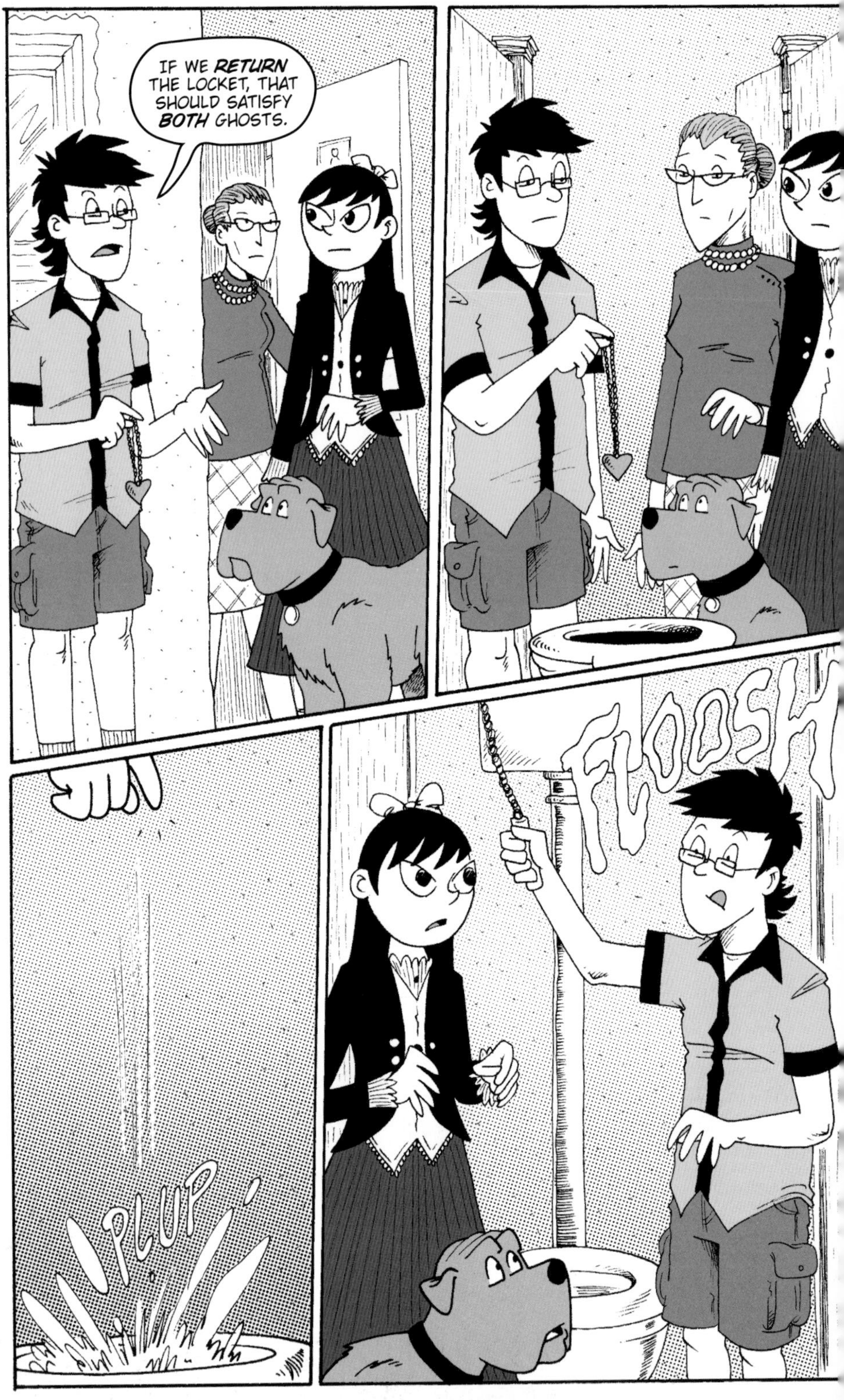
IF WE RETURN THE LOCKET, THAT SHOULD SATISFY BOTH GHOSTS.
PLUP
FLOOSH

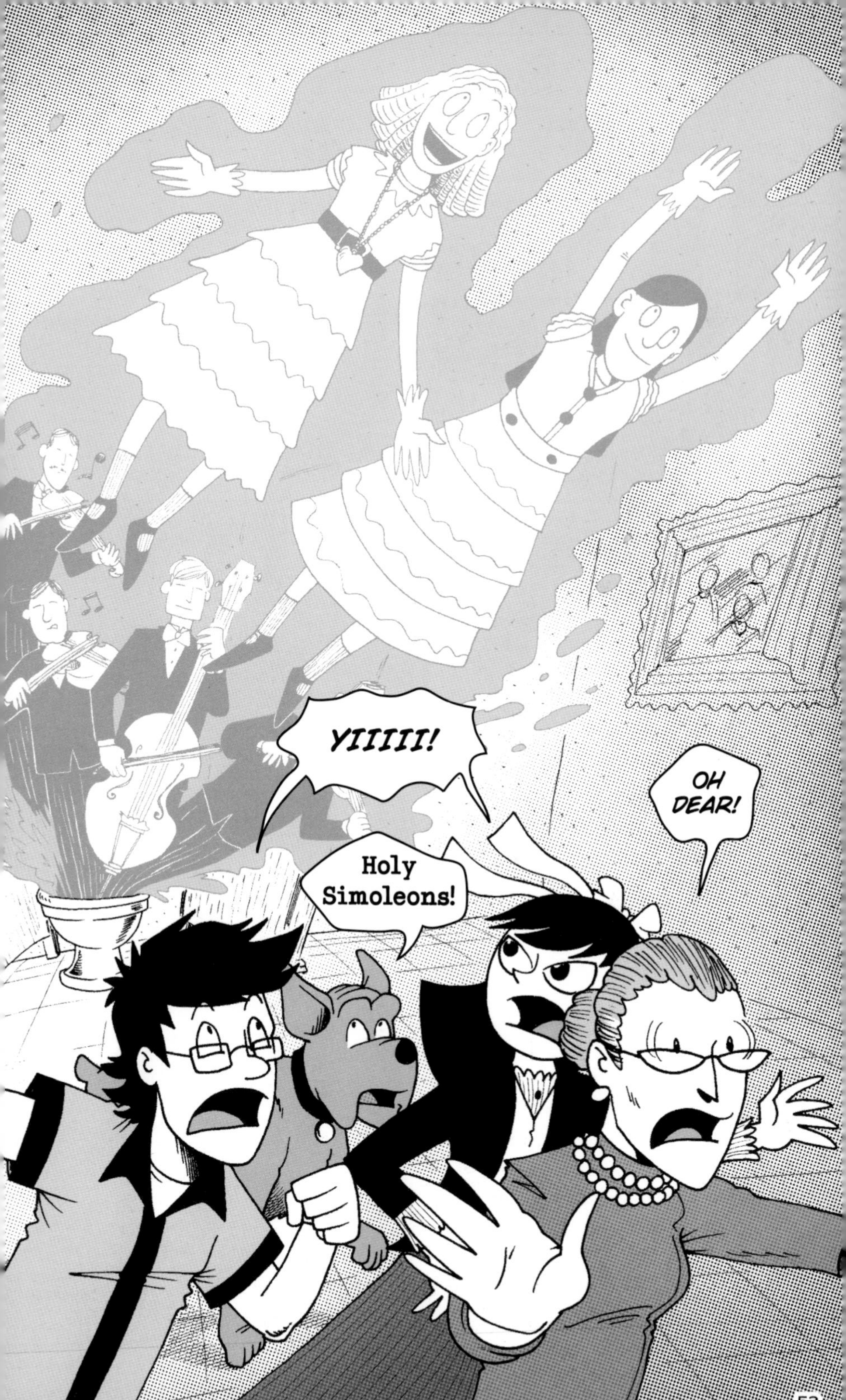
YIIIII!
OH DEAR!
Holy Simoleons!

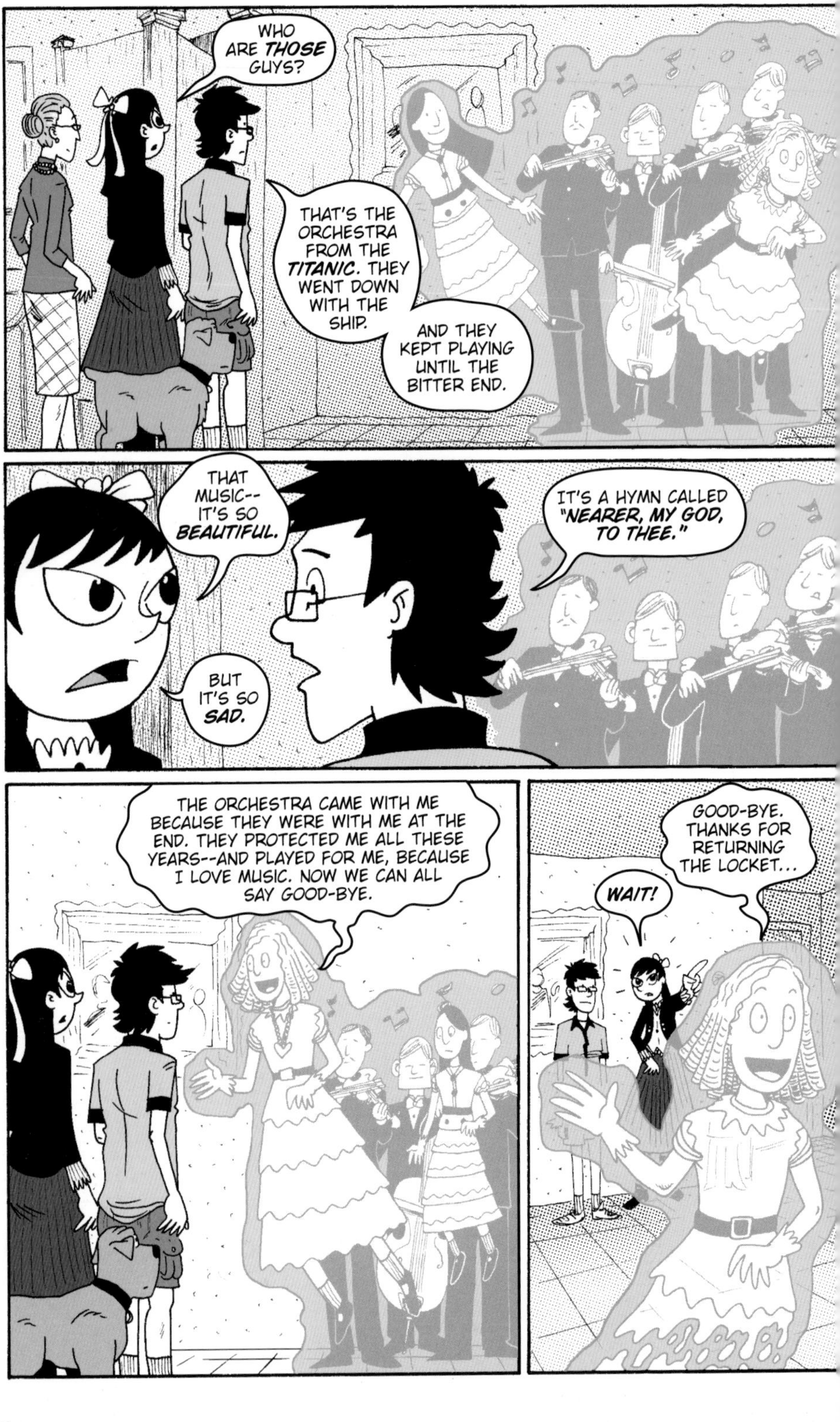
WHO ARE THOSE GUYS?
THAT'S THE ORCHESTRA FROM THE TITANIC. THEY WENT DOWN WITH THE SHIP.
AND THEY KEPT PLAYING UNTIL THE BITTER END.
THAT MUSIC-- IT'S SO BEAUTIFUL.
BUT IT'S SO SAD.
IT'S A HYMN CALLED "NEARER, MY GOD, TO THEE."
THE ORCHESTRA CAME WITH ME BECAUSE THEY WERE WITH ME AT THE END. THEY PROTECTED ME ALL THESE YEARS--AND PLAYED FOR ME, BECAUSE I LOVE MUSIC. NOW WE CAN ALL SAY GOOD-BYE.
GOOD-BYE. THANKS FOR RETURNING THE LOCKET...
WAIT!

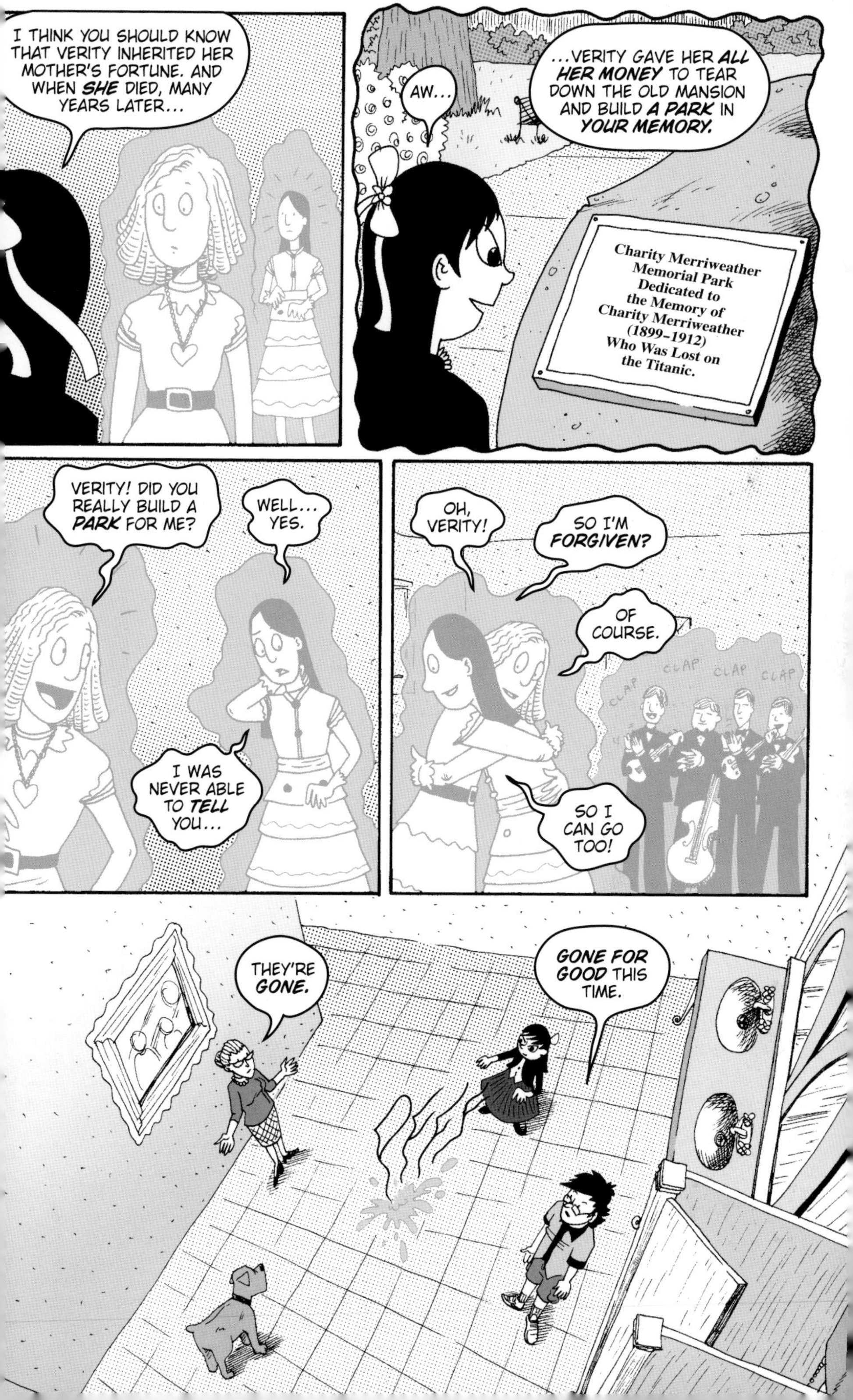
I THINK YOU SHOULD KNOW THAT VERITY INHERITED HER MOTHER'S FORTUNE. AND WHEN SHE DIED, MANY YEARS LATER...
AW...
...VERITY GAVE HER ALL HER MONEY TO TEAR DOWN THE OLD MANSION AND BUILD A PARK IN YOUR MEMORY.
Charity Merriweather Memorial Park Dedicated to the Memory of Charity Merriweather (1899–1912) Who Was Lost on the Titanic.
VERITY! DID YOU REALLY BUILD A PARK FOR ME?
WELL... YES.
I WAS NEVER ABLE TO TELL YOU...
OH, VERITY!
SO I'M FORGIVEN?
OF COURSE.
CLAP CLAP CLAP CLAP
SO I CAN GO TOO!
THEY'RE GONE.
GONE FOR GOOD THIS TIME.

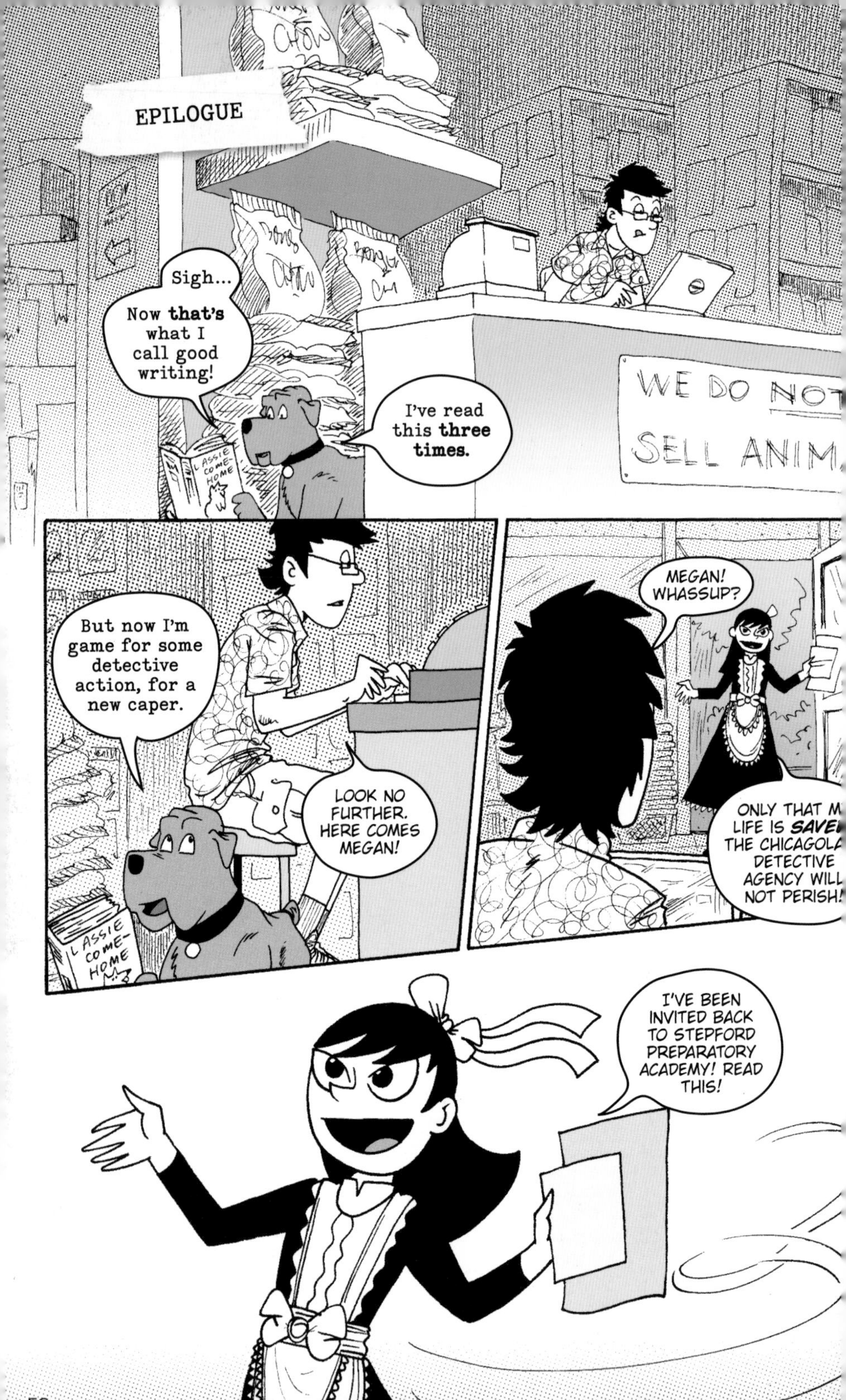

EPILOGUE
Sigh... Now **that's** what I call good writing!
I've read this **three times.**
WE DO NOT SELL ANIM
LASSIE COME-HOME
But now I'm game for some detective action, for a new caper.
LOOK NO FURTHER. HERE COMES MEGAN!
LASSIE COME-HOME
MEGAN! WHASSUP?
ONLY THAT M LIFE IS ***SAVE*** THE CHICAGOLA DETECTIVE AGENCY WILL NOT PERISH!
I'VE BEEN INVITED BACK TO STEPFORD PREPARATORY ACADEMY! READ THIS!

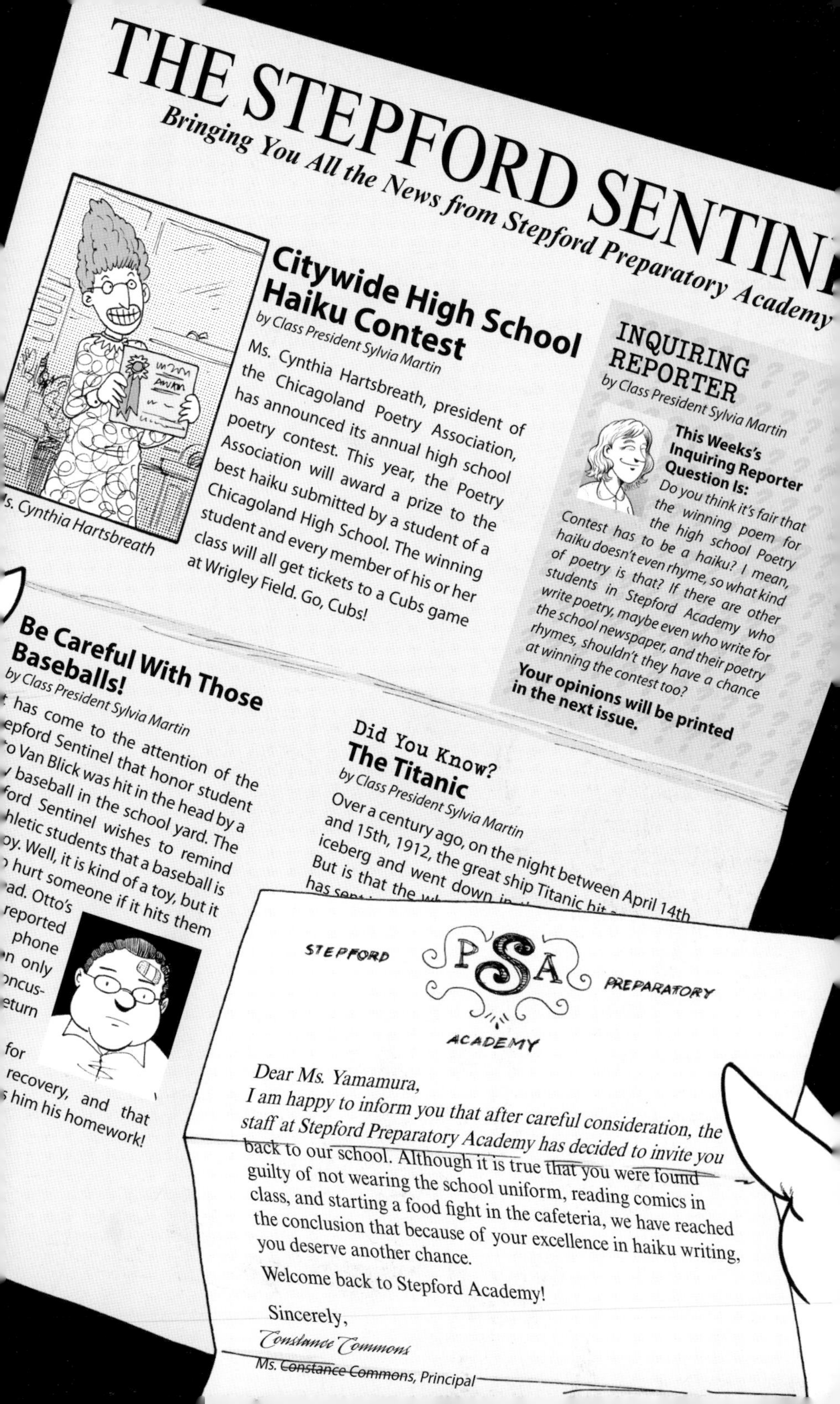

THE STEPFORD SENTIN

Bringing You All the News from Stepford Preparatory Academy

s. Cynthia Hartsbreath

Citywide High School Haiku Contest

by Class President Sylvia Martin

Ms. Cynthia Hartsbreath, president of the Chicagoland Poetry Association, has announced its annual high school poetry contest. This year, the Poetry Association will award a prize to the best haiku submitted by a student of a Chicagoland High School. The winning student and every member of his or her class will all get tickets to a Cubs game at Wrigley Field. Go, Cubs!

INQUIRING REPORTER

by Class President Sylvia Martin

This Weeks's Inquiring Reporter Question Is:

Do you think it's fair that the winning poem for the high school Poetry Contest has to be a haiku? I mean, haiku doesn't even rhyme, so what kind of poetry is that? If there are other students in Stepford Academy who write poetry, maybe even who write for the school newspaper, and their poetry rhymes, shouldn't they have a chance at winning the contest too?

Your opinions will be printed in the next issue.

Be Careful With Those Baseballs!

by Class President Sylvia Martin

: has come to the attention of the
epford Sentinel that honor student
o Van Blick was hit in the head by a
/ baseball in the school yard. The
ord Sentinel wishes to remind
hletic students that a baseball is
oy. Well, it is kind of a toy, but it
hurt someone if it hits them
ad. Otto's
reported
phone
n only
oncus-
eturn
for
recovery, and that
s him his homework!

Did You Know?

The Titanic

by Class President Sylvia Martin

Over a century ago, on the night between April 14th and 15th, 1912, the great ship Titanic hit
iceberg and went down
But is that the
has sen

STEPFORD PSA PREPARATORY ACADEMY

Dear Ms. Yamamura,

I am happy to inform you that after careful consideration, the staff at Stepford Preparatory Academy has decided to invite you back to our school. Although it is true that you were found guilty of not wearing the school uniform, reading comics in class, and starting a food fight in the cafeteria, we have reached the conclusion that because of your excellence in haiku writing, you deserve another chance.

Welcome back to Stepford Academy!

Sincerely,

Constance Commons

Ms. Constance Commons, Principal

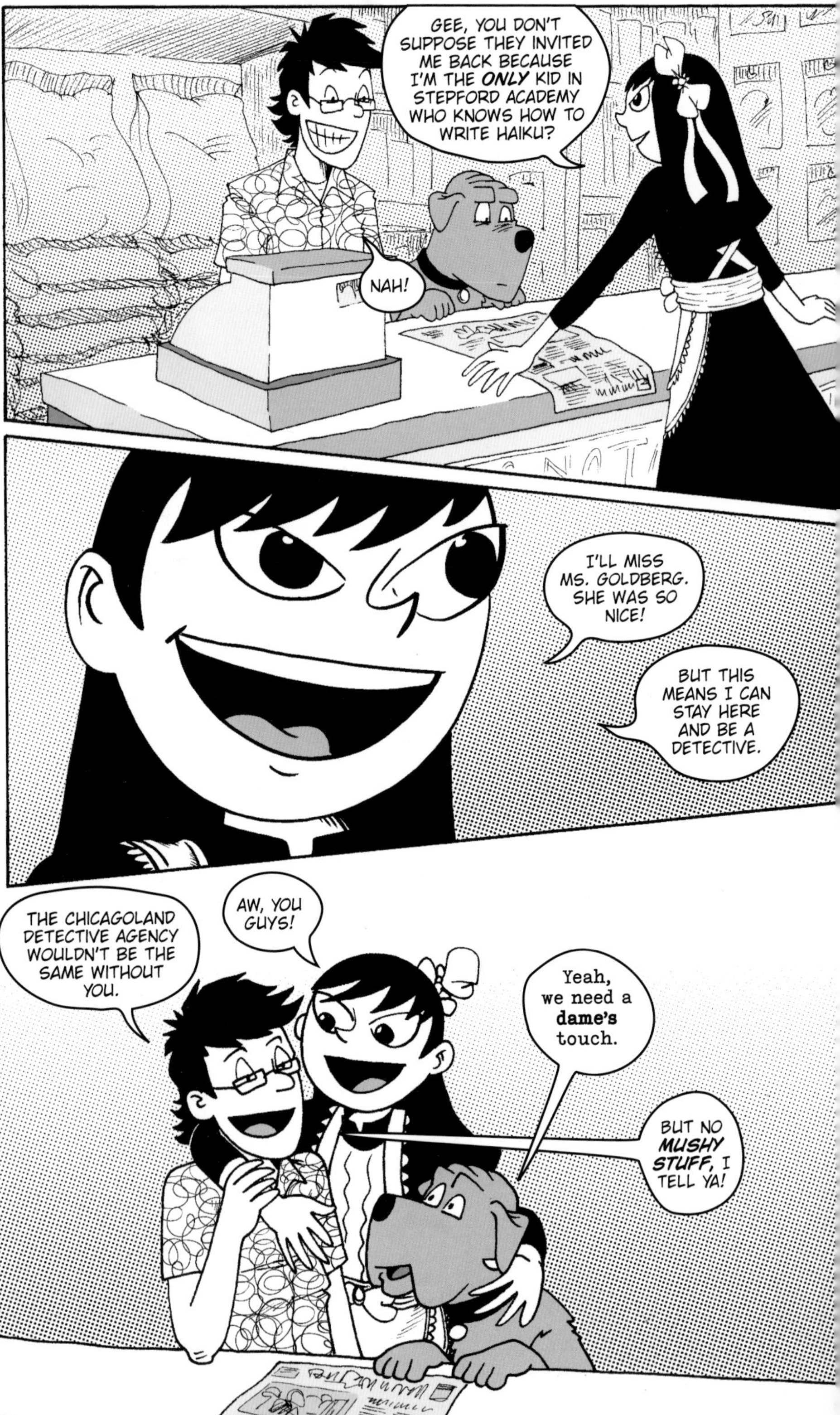
GEE, YOU DON'T SUPPOSE THEY INVITED ME BACK BECAUSE I'M THE ONLY KID IN STEPFORD ACADEMY WHO KNOWS HOW TO WRITE HAIKU?
NAH!
I'LL MISS MS. GOLDBERG. SHE WAS SO NICE!
BUT THIS MEANS I CAN STAY HERE AND BE A DETECTIVE.
THE CHICAGOLAND DETECTIVE AGENCY WOULDN'T BE THE SAME WITHOUT YOU.
AW, YOU GUYS!
Yeah, we need a dame's touch.
BUT NO MUSHY STUFF, I TELL YA!

CHICAGO KIDS HAVE BIG DAY AT BALLPARK

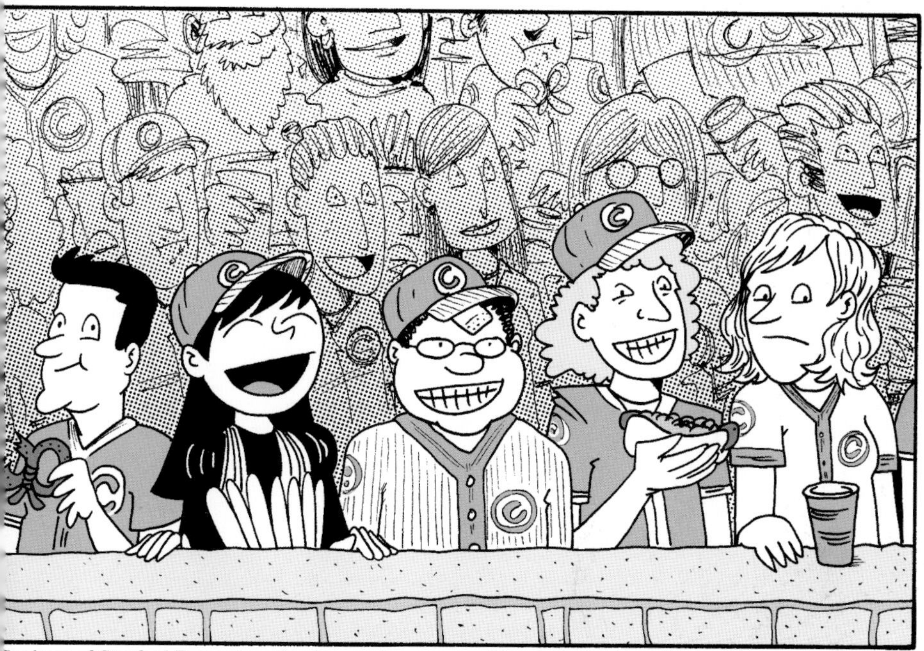

Students of Stepford Preparatory Academy enjoy a game of baseball, thanks to Megan Yamamura, second from left, who won first prize in the citywide haiku contest. The prize was a trip to the ballpark for her entire class. Fifteen minutes after this photo was taken, Otto Van Blick, third from left, was hit on the nose while attempting to catch a fly ball.

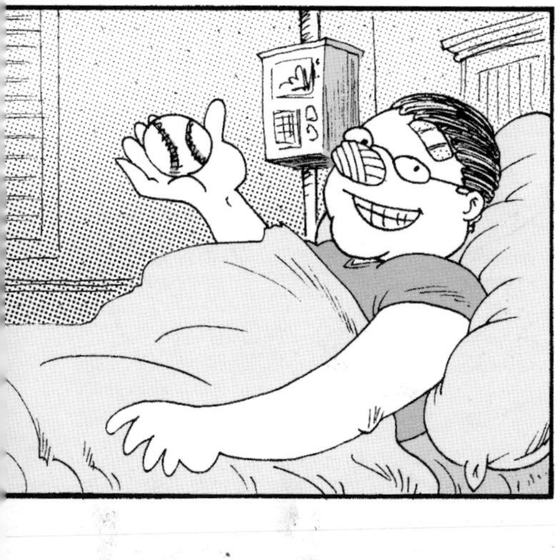

Boy Clonked in Nose by Fly Ball

Otto Van Blick, a freshman at Stepford Preparatory Academy, holds up the fly ball he almost caught at yesterday's big game. Otto broke his nose trying to catch the ball but was released from the hospital after his nose was bandaged. The team gave him the ball anyway and autographed it for him.

Student's Winning Haiku

A boy, a big dog,
Nothing too weird for those guys.
My friends forever.

—by Megan Yamamura

MYBLOGFACE

CHICAGOLAND DETECTIVE AGENCY

InforFACEtion

Location: Behind the counter of Hernandez & Sons Pet Supply store

Hours: 9–5 during summer vacation. During the rest of the year, after school hours, except on weekends

Bring your pets. We love animals, and we barter!

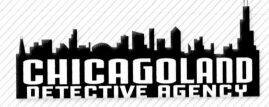

Our motto:

Stumped? Scared? Need help fast?
Chicagoland Detectives:
No case is too weird.

In case you're wondering, our motto is in haiku form. Haiku is an ancient Japanese form of poetry, written in 3 lines. The first and last lines have 5 syllables, and the middle line has 7 syllables. Our haiku was composed by poet and special agent Megan Yamamura, who invites you to try writing your own haiku.

Meet the FACE

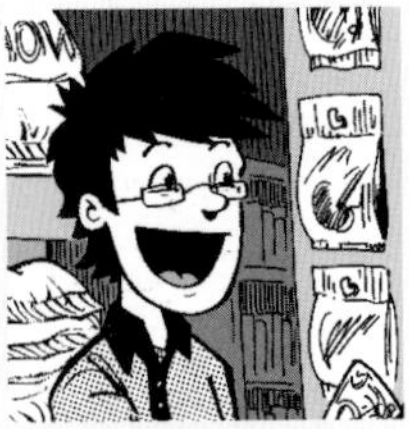

Raf Hernandez

Age: 12

Education: James A. Garfield Middle School

MyBlogFace Likes

Likes

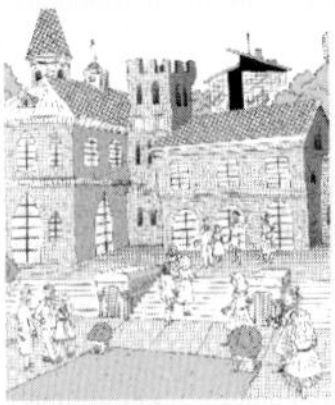

Pine Lake Academy

Chicagoland BLOG ENTRY #4

By Raf Hernandez

The wreck of the *Titanic* was one of the biggest disasters in modern history. But here's more about the year 1912:

In 1912, you could count the number of women pilots on one hand, but one of the most famous was Harriet Quimby. On April 16, one day after the *Titanic* disaster, she became the first woman to fly the English Channel. She had only received her pilot's license the year before!

Movies were big and getting bigger. In those pre-TV days, rich American families could watch movies in their living rooms on something called the Home Kinetoscope.

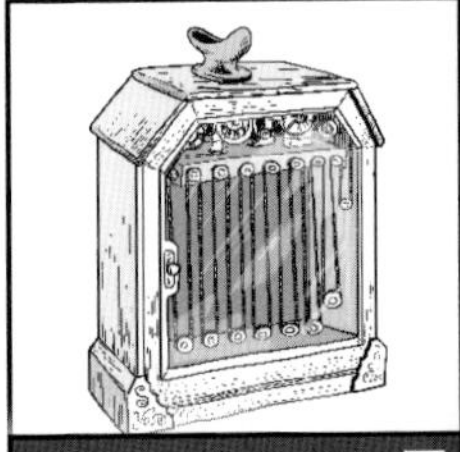

Kinetoscope

Or they could go out to watch movies featuring Charlie Chaplin and Mary Pickford, at the nickelodeon, a small movie theater, for the price of five cents, one nickel. (And that's why they were called nickelodeons!) Plus, 1912 was the first year that popcorn was sold at movie theaters.

You should check out some old Charlie Chaplin movies--he's still funny, a century later. Mary Pickford is something else. She had long curls and wore fluffy little dresses, and they called her America's Sweetheart. But she was so sweet it made your teeth ache--and she was still playing little girls when she was in her twenties!

MYBLOGFACE

New FACE Friend

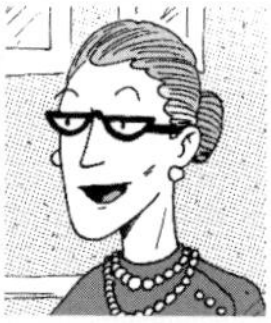

Ms. Greta Goldberg, Headmistress of Pine Lake Academy

Chicagoland BLOG ENTRY #4 Continued

"Alexander's Ragtime Band" was the biggest hit song of the year, but some other popular songs that people were humming were "When Irish Eyes Are Smiling," "Be My Little Baby Bumblebee," and "Ragtime Cowboy Joe." In 1912, you bought those songs on big heavy 78 rpm records and played them on windup Victrolas. Today you can easily find them on the Internet.

For my next project, I'm experimenting with combining computer-generated music with a ragtime beat to produce a new kind of music, called ***Raftime***!

Guest Blogger: Megan Yamamura

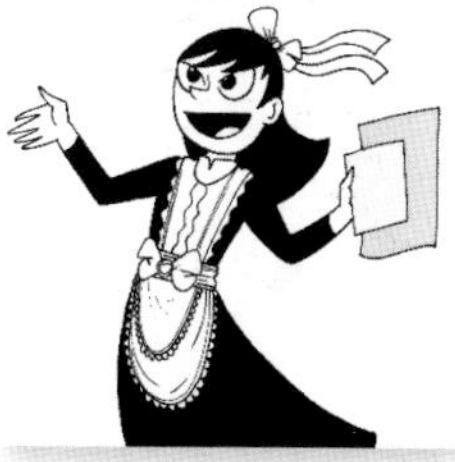

I want to tell you about my wardrobe. My dresses are made by a company called ***Baby the Moon Shines Bright***. It's a Japanese dress company, and the style of dress they make is called Lolita. It's a Victorian-looking style that reminds me of tea parties and haunted houses, which is awesome because I love haunted houses and tea parties. There are tons of variations on the Lolita style, like Alice Lolita, which is inspired by *Alice in Wonderland*; Country Lolita, which features straw baskets and hats, fruit and checked patterns; and Pirate Lolita (guess what that's inspired by!). But the elegant black Lolita dresses are called Gothic Lolita. I think black is very soulful and poetic and expresses the deep hidden sorrow of a teenage girl, so that's why I wear it.

There are other companies that make Lolita dresses, but my favorite is ***Baby the Moon Shines Bright***. They have stores in Tokyo, Paris, and San Francisco, but none in Chicagoland, which means I have to buy my dresses over the Internet. The dresses are sort of expensive, and my clueless dad, who has no idea that these dresses are the most important thing in the world, objects to the price, so sometimes I have to use my allowance to pay for them. This is a problem, because usually I have spent all my allowance on manga. I think the Chicagoland Detective Agency needs to find some real paying clients!

MYBLOGFACE

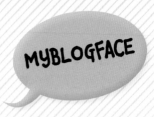

CHICAGOLAND
DETECTIVE AGENCY

Meet the FACE

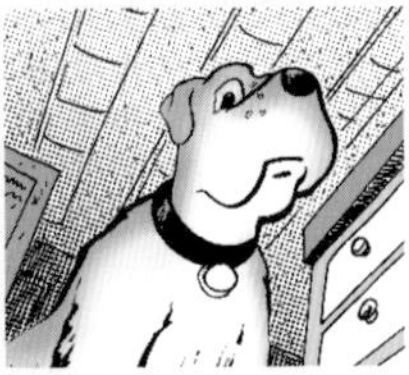

Bradley
Age: 2
Motto: A dog's gotta do what a dog's gotta do

Friendly FACErs

6 Friends

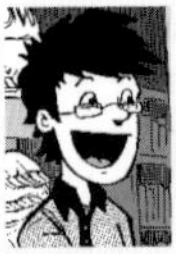

Raf Hernandez

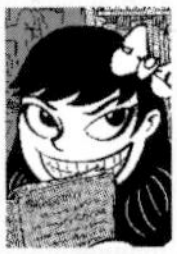

Megan Yamamura

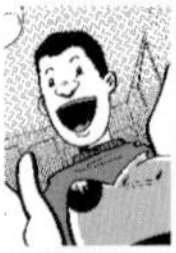

William Johnson

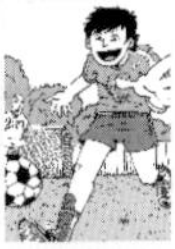

Davey Kanaris

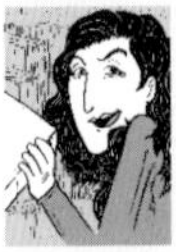

Rhonda Kanaris

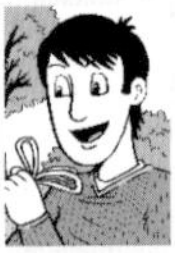

Jimmy Papadopoulis

Guest Blogger: Bradley

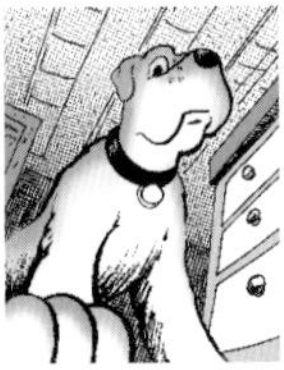

I want to apologize to my service dog brothers and sisters, because I pretended to be one of them so that I could enter Pine Lake Academy and again so that I could ride the bus with Raf and Megan. And it's only because I am a doggie Einstein that I could pull it off. Real service dogs are very smart (even though not as smart as me) and very well trained to help disabled people. As puppies, they are sent to live with a foster family that teaches them basic dog politeness skills like waiting at doors, riding in cars, coming when called, walking on a leash, and not begging or jumping on people.

After that, only the best go on to further training. Dogs are individually trained to help the person they're gonna be working with. You might have thought that service dogs only helped blind people, but they do so much more! There are dogs who hear for deaf people and dogs who help people in wheelchairs by opening and closing doors for them, picking up stuff they drop, and turning lights on and off.

Being a service dog is the most noble profession a doggie can aspire to, and if I were not a master detective, I would want to be a service dog.

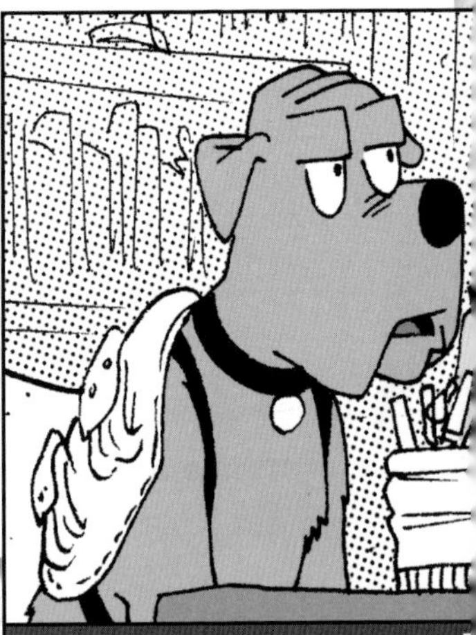

Bradley in service dog jacket

ABOUT THE AUTHOR AND ILLUSTRATOR

TRINA ROBBINS, an Eisner Award and Harvey Award nominee, made a name for herself in the underground comix movement of the 1960s. She published the first all-woman comic book in the 1970s; published her first history of women cartoonists, *Women and the Comics*, in the 1980s; was an artist for the *Wonder Woman* comic book; and created the superhero series *Go Girl!* with artist Anne Timmons. And that's just a start—she has written biographies, other nonfiction, and way too many other books and comics for kids and adults to list, but you can check them out on her website at www.trinarobbins.com. She lives in San Francisco with her partner, comics artist Steve Leialoha.

TYLER PAGE is an Eisner Award-nominated illustrator and webcomic artist who has self-published four graphic novels, including *Nothing Better*, recipient of a Xeric Foundation Grant. His day job is director of Print Technology at the Minneapolis College of Art and Design, where he oversees the college's print-based facilities. He's been drawing his whole life and sometime around middle school started making his own comics starring the family cat. He lives with wife Cori Doerrfeld, daughter Charlotte, and two crazy cats in Minneapolis, and his website lives at www.stylishvittles.com.

STUMPED? SCARED? NEED HELP FAST?

CHICAGOLAND DETECTIVE AGENCY CAN DO THE JOB.

NO CASE TOO WEIRD!

It can't get much weirder than this: Raf, Megan, and Bradley have been abducted by aliens from the planet Farf III! These are not your ordinary, everyday aliens, either. They're intelligent canines who can speak, just like Bradley. The Farfian princess has gone missing, and the space-dogs need help from planet Earth's home team—the Chicagoland Detective Agency—to track her down.

This is a case Bradley can really sink his teeth into. But will his loyalty to his human friends prove more powerful than the chance to live where it's the two-legged people who are the pets?

The investigation into this interstellar caper will be launched in . . .

CHICAGOLAND DETECTIVE AGENCY #5

THE BARK IN SPACE

BY TRINA ROBBINS

ILLUSTRATED BY TYLER PAGE